Christmas Connections

miracles one good deed at a time

Halene Petersen Dahlstrom

Publication Consultants

PO Box 221974 Anchorage, Alaska 99522-1974

ISBN 1-888125-70-5

Library of Congress Catalog Card Number: 00-105348

Copyright 2000 by Halene Petersen Dahlstrom
—First Edition—
—First Printing 2000—
—Second Printing 2001—

Manufactured in the United States of America.

Dedication

This book is dedicated to my mother, Harriet H. Petersen, who taught me to love words at an early age, that determination is half the battle, and the importance of being true to one's convictions.

To my dad, Loyd B. Petersen (Pa Pete), for his examples of creativity, humor and the ability to reach beyond self in service to others.

To my husband, Dan, and our children: Jeff, Kati, Colter and Jennalee, for times of patient support, serving as sounding boards, providing comic relief, and for not giving up on a dream that they didn't always understand.

And, to Heavenly Father for allowing this book to be one of my Life Challenges.

Table of Contents

Acknowledgments

To all family members, friends and associates who encouraged, inspired, proofread, critiqued, provided details or computer assistance — gratitude beyond words.

Especially to: Mom, Merrell, and Nadene Dahlstrom, Joel'lene Anderson, Thera Bagley, Dr. Rick Braun, Kathy Brown, Susann Bustemante, Kathleen Carter, Debbie Cartwright, Vilma Chavez, Laurie Christensen, RaeAnna Christensen, Wendy Christensen, Julie P. and George A. Dansie Sr., Julie Lynn Dansie, Sara Ellis, Christine Forbes, Cheryl Forchuk, Carol Franklin, Cindy Hutchinson, Ardeth G. Kapp, Patricia Kilson, Helen Lobato, Dario Lugo, Joy McDonald, Kathy McLean, Susan A.T. Mundy, Elaine Petersen, Nina Petersen, Sherry Peterson, Eileen Rich, Kim Roeder, Kristine P. Smith, Marie Turner, Bonnie Wells, and Lola C. Wilson.

Computer Cavalry: David, John-David, and Nick Anderson, Quinton Christensen, George Dansie Jr., Russ Hansen, Bob Thompson, and assorted missionaries.

Also, Marthy Johnson, editor, and Evan and Margaret Swensen of Publishing Consultants for finally waving the wand.

Posthumously to: Dad, Berdell, and others beyond …

Apologies to anyone I may have inadvertently forgotten.

Preface

Once upon a time, in a part of the 60s that wasn't about hippies or protests or experimentation, there was a place called Hometown. It was a place soldiers longed for, high school kids cheered for, and the restless ran away from only to be drawn back time and again. It was an easy place to find, nestled snugly among other such towns, not too far from The City. So what made it unique?

Perhaps it was a sense of security; of belonging. Or maybe the way it was wrapped around the lives of those who lived there, like a warm flannel blanket on a chilly evening. In either case, Hometown was about the people who lived there. What they gave to it or took from it ultimately determined its character, added to its texture, its colors, its connections.

Christmastime 1965 brought some unforeseen connections to Hometown. One particular link was started by a 12-year-old girl named Suzannah Brown, because of a special Christmas wish, and her determination to see it come true. With a little help from Heaven. Some call it inspiration. Some call it luck. Some see it in small things. Some don't recognize it at all. But from a distance, another family member pleaded for Suzannah to succeed. Her own future, her earthly existence depended on it.

Heaven

The last sound of Heaven that you hear before you leave is music. Not a tinkling note, but an ever-present musical wave that floods each soul it enfolds with captivating melodies. Celestial choirs of angels, and spirits from generations past and future raise a vocal tribute of love and encouragement to those beginning their earthly journey.

The spirit child shivered with joy as the hallowed harmonies resonated throughout the courtyard and tickled the fibers of her being. Oh she loved the music so! If only they sang for her!

Too tiny to see over the polished rail, she peered between the sculpted lower posts of a balcony, and watched longingly as another premortal playmate entered the crystalline courtyard below. Her little companion paused briefly to wave before crossing the rainbow-flecked floor, and then timidly approached the celestial throne.

The Interviewer looked up at the spirit child, smiled warmly, then beckoned her friend to His side. Lovingly, He drew that one near and whispered Life Challenges into her ear. She nodded shyly. He kissed her forehead, and then motioned for her escort to lead her to the golden staircase leading down to the Crossing Corridor.

Favorite friend gone, the spirit child wistfully meandered down silver-trimmed stairways and galleried halls until she passed through the archway and exited the majestic rotunda.

She passed many pleasant souls on her way to the nearest garden. Each seemed to have a sense of purpose or destination. Some hurried off to teach. Others rushed off to *learn. Some composed music. Others listened appreciatively. Some conversed about life. Others painted or wrote. Her own escort was reading near the hyacinths.*

The little spirit sat down on the warm, fragrant grass in such a huff that the wide sash on her delicate gossamer gown poofed upward, then drifted gently into place beside her.

The escort looked up from her book. "How was it?"

"Wonderful." she sighed, resignedly.

"How did she look?"

"Happy."

"And how was the music?"

"More than beautiful. It just wasn't for me." Another heavy sigh.

"They said 'no' again?"

The little spirit nodded her head slowly. "I still have to wait. It's not fair, Ginny!"

Ginny closed her book. "I know you're disappointed, but these things happen sometimes. It could be about choices. It could be about challenges. Things don't often go as planned down there."

"Did they forget me?"

"Not knowingly, but it's easy to forget there. They get wrapped up in earthly concerns."

The spirit child groaned.

Ginny stood, smoothing the folds of her satin caftan and held out her hand. "I think we should make a visit to the viewing place to see what the delay is about. I have asked for permission, and if the timing is right, it may be allowed."

For a moment the spirit child did not comprehend what had been suggested. Suddenly her eyes brightened. "Could we see them? Could we really see?"

"We can ask to see."

These words had barely been offered when the spirit child enthusiastically grabbed hold of Ginny's hand and half-dragging, pulled her across the wide, lush lawn, like a tawny pony straining at its reins.

Walking along pearl-pebbled paths, their swishing robes and tick-clicking slippers created a rhythm to the rhyme of songs they could hear in the distance. Leaving through the garden's southern gate, they crossed a marbled courtyard, greeting many as they passed, till they reached the pillared entrance of an immense structure. Awestruck, the spirit child paused. Ginny reassuringly squeezed the little hand and led her companion along an azure-tiled hallway until they reached the circular center of the building.

"An Observation Portal, please," Ginny requested of the Greeter.

He looked briefly into a gilt-edged book, and then directed them to one of many shimmering screens that encircled the room.

"What do we do now?" the spirit child whispered excitedly, gazing at the glistening formation that was as tall as Ginny, and wider than both of her own arms outstretched.

"We see what day it is," Ginny answered, barely touching the lower right corner. A date and location caption appeared.

*G*inny knelt down, taking both of the spirit child's hands in hers. "Now, think about whom you want to see."

The spirit child closed her eyes tightly and repeated aloud, "My family. My family. My family."

Soon a large picture appeared.

Hometown, 3:30 p.m.

"Fine! Stay here feeling sorry for yourself if you want to!" Carol Brown shouted through the door of the old stucco duplex. "I'm taking Suzannah shopping, and we're gonna have *fun!*"

Still muttering, she stomped down the porch, got into their dark green '58 Fairlane and slammed the door. She opened her mouth, ready to express some further exasperations, but was stopped short by the wide-eyed, questioning glance of her daughter, who had heard her yell before, and seen her slam before, but never both together, nor so defiantly. Carol took a deep breath, exhaled slowly, then said, "I guess it's just you and me tonight, kiddo. Dad's sort of … busy."

"Oh dear. That could explain it," Ginny said.

"What?" the spirit child asked, eagerly.

"Well, little one, it seems that your folks aren't getting along."

"But they love each other! They held hands and promised to send for us ... so we could be a family."

"I'm sure they still love each other. But they don't remember. They must have sensed the divine spark when they met again on earth, and kept feeling it until it was drowned by earthly cares or ... taken for granted. When this happens, and people realize something is missing, they often begin to doubt the spark was there in the first place. If this has happened to your parents it makes continuing their married life more difficult and makes beginning your new life nearly impossible."

"What am I going to do?"

"There's not much we can do. We can't read thoughts, or interfere in any way without permission. What we need is more information, so for now, we're going to wait, watch and hope."

The little spirit whimpered. The picture and caption changed.

Woodland Road, 3:40 p.m.

The excitement of the week before Christmas danced as wildly around Suzannah Brown as the millions of fanciful snowflakes that tumbled and swirled through the darkening sky. Eyes mesmerized by every detail she could see through the window, she clasped her mittened hands together, as if squeezing them tightly would hold anticipation at bay.

She was a 12-year-old with a mission. This year she was choosing gifts for her parents personally. It might not seem like much to others but Suzannah had saved money since her birthday, September 1, and couldn't wait to spend it.

In previous years, her parents had each taken her secretly aside, handed her something from Bud's Bargain-All to wrap and said, "This is for you to give to Mom." Or, "This is what you got for Daddy."

And that was fine. It hadn't bothered her that the gifts weren't much of a surprise for them because hey, she was a kid. She didn't have any money, and was usually too keyed up wondering what *she* was going to receive on Christmas morning to let it worry her.

This year would be different. After all, she was twelve now and she had a plan. She also had seven dollars and eighty-eight cents and her good luck ribbon tied around her dark auburn ponytail.

As they drove past the Bargain-All, Suzannah thought about her shopping experience a few days earlier. She had tried to find the perfect gifts there, not knowing exactly what she was looking for, just trusting that she would recognize them when she saw them. Unfortunately, she couldn't find a thing, which was amazing given the fact that Bud's little Hometown corner store had nearly everything you'd ever need or want packed into shelves from floor to ceiling. Gloves, galoshes, hats, handbags, scarves, shirts, shoes, rakes, rows of fabric, thread, bread, patterns, lanterns, and Twirl-Town Toys all had a spot to fill. Not to mention the two front corner coolers that held milk, eggs and semi-limp lettuce, cabbage or carrots. However, after an hour of looking up and down through all the crammed, winding aisles, the only thing Suzannah came out with was a stiff neck and twelve cents worth of the best penny candy in the valley.

Not discouraged, she had sweetly convinced her mom to venture the following weekend into Mayville fifteen miles away; something they usually didn't do except to the J.C. Penney's back-to-school sales, or at Easter time for a new spring dress and sandals. But Suzannah was aching to look in Denton's Five and Dime for the much-needed perfect presents. Amazingly, her mother seemed to like the idea of this Christmas trek and had hoped they might coax Dad to go along, thinking it might lift his sagging spirits to look at Christmas lights on the houses and shops along their way home.

That part of the plan had obviously fizzled with her parents' latest argument, so after giving her mom a few minutes to collect her thoughts, and get underway, Suzannah unfolded the second part of her plan. Casually, she asked, "Were you going to do any *other* shopping?"

There was no answer. Mom's concentrating on her driving, Suzannah figured. Woodland Road was becoming slicker by the mile.

Actually, Carol Brown was still mentally standing on the porch at home yelling a few other bottled-up frustrations through the duplex door. No wonder her light brown hair had sprouted a few gray strays! Perhaps some justice came from knowing that her husband's wavy rust-colored locks were thinning prematurely too. She almost laughed, then was awash in despair. What a pathetic thing to find amusement in! It was all she could do to fight back the tears and swallow the emotional crush of her throat. It took her brain several seconds to register Susannah's question. Finally she asked, "What was that?"

Suzannah repeated the question, using her best casual tone of voice, trying not to raise suspicion. "I said … were you going to do any *other* shopping, you know, other than at Denton's?"

"Why?"

"Just wondering."

Carol let it drop momentarily, feeling inside the pocket of her purple-trimmed, nubby-tweed coat in hopes of finding a tissue, knowing also that the silence wouldn't last. She was right.

Before they reached South Wadimoor four miles down the road, Suzannah shifted in her seat, fidgeted with the red, barrel-shaped buttons on her navy blue corduroy coat, then blurted out, "Well, because maybe if you were going to do some other shopping, you could sort of drop me off for a few minutes, and I could be looking around to see what I want. You know, to add on my Christmas list."

As she said it, Suzannah's inward groans rumbled so loudly that her stomach reeled from holding the commotion. *Her* Christmas list had been handed in a month ago; a couple of new records for her hand-me-down hi fi, a locket or necklace, a new flannel nightgown and a dog.

Of course, she couldn't get the dog because they were renting in Mr. Metzler's ancient two-bedroom duplex, and he hated pets! Although every time the shared furnace kicked in, it sure smelled like he had a cat. Still there was no sense arguing about it. For now a dog was out of the question. Surely her folks would find some nice surprise to fill in the blank. Now, because of her nervous chatter, her mom would think she was getting greedy and expected to be given a lot more. Brother! She wasn't an expert on this surprise business and sure hoped that her mom would take the hint. Which she did.

"I guess I could go next door to the drugstore for ten minutes, then come find you."

A surge of relief splashed through Suzannah from shoe to scarf. "Great!" she squeaked, struggled to clear her throat, then finagled a bit more, "And if they're really busy and it takes fifteen minutes, that's okay. I won't go anywhere else. I'll stay right there. I could even meet you by the candy counter, in twenty minutes or so?"

"Do you really think you'll need that long? I can only give you three dollars, honey. We agreed to cut back this year because Daddy got laid off from the mine," Carol Brown apologized, pulling into a space in the back parking lot that connected the two stores. "I know it's not much. If you want, you can get Daddy something and draw me one of your neat pictures."

The bottled-up groan escaped. "Mother! I'm not going to draw you a dumb picture!" she protested, then kissed her mother on the cheek. "See you in half an hour," she giggled, and bounced out of the car, flipping the hood of her coat into place on her head as she went.

"Suz, you didn't take any money!"

"It's okay," Suzannah called back over her shoulder, as she scampered carefully across the parking lot, trying hard not to fall on the ice. A Chrysler Crown Imperial pulled up to the curb in front of the U-Save Drugstore. It was that neat burgundy color that Suzannah liked; other than that, she paid little attention to it.

The moment she stepped into Denton's Five and Dime she was entranced by the magical combination of twinkling lights, merry music, and the scrumptious smell of roasting cashews so thick in the air she could taste it. The mittens went into one pocket, and her tooled-leather coin purse came out of the other. She took a deep breath. On your mark, get set ...go!

Suzannah knew where she was headed—right up to the cosmetics counter. She knew what her parents needed … Laughter! Romance! *Perfume!* She'd seen ads in magazines and on TV and was determined to find an amorous one for her mom. Maybe it would help her folks stop arguing, and her dad would lighten up and joke around again. Maybe he'd even dance her mom around the kitchen when the Lawrence Welk Show came on, or get that silly grin on his face and sneak a kiss to the back of her neck while she fixed dinner; the kinds of things he'd done months before, before the job problem, before the arguing, when they used to be in love. The remedy seemed so simple she wondered why her parents hadn't thought of it themselves. Nevermind, she would take care of it.

The picture appearing next on the silken screen was that of a man and woman sitting in a burgundy-colored automobile.

"What happened to Suzannah?" the spirit child cried out.

"Just because you can't see her doesn't mean she's not there. Very little of what we do in life affects only us. Sometimes the connections we make help us on our journey, and sometimes our journey helps others begin a journey of their own. Apparently Suzannah is going to need help from other sources. This may be one of those sources."

"It's getting so complicated."

"Life often does. Don't give up because you can't see the full picture right now."

The spirit child's gaze returned to the picture of the man and woman in the car.

Mayville, 4:15 p.m.

"Ready?" Patricia's husband, Robert asked, cautiously.

She took a slow, deep breath. "I'm waiting until that little girl goes into the store, then the coast will be clear. There's less of a chance of being recognized."

"In that get-up?" Robert asked, smiling broadly.

"Yes! What if *he* shows up?"

"He won't. He goes to the Legion Hall on Saturday nights. Besides, even *he* wouldn't recognize you in this disguise."

"I wish there was another place." Patricia's voice trailed off.

"Sorry hon, this is where the Center could arrange it on such short notice. You'll do all right. I'll get it set up for ya," Robert encouraged, then bounded out of the car with far more enthusiasm than Patricia thought appropriate for the situation.

"I can't believe I am actually doing this," Patricia mumbled, disgusted, and made a quick mental review of the events of recent days that led up to this, the most humiliating experience she would ever embark upon in her life.

It had all started in The City, the previous Wednesday afternoon. Patricia was waiting for Robert outside the Imperial Gardens Restaurant. They were going to meet for a romantic little lunch, but as usual, he was late. She decided not to ruin the mood by being impatient with him. It was nearly Christmas and she didn't want to antagonize him. Afterward she would suggest that they walk through Bachman's department store just to look at the lovely decorations, as they did every year at Christmas. Then she'd nonchalantly steer Robert toward the fur department. She had desperately wanted him to see the blue fox jacket on display. It was incredibly beautiful, and had looked absolutely fabulous on her when she tried it on earlier in the week. She hoped Robert would take the hint.

It wasn't that Robert didn't want to give her nice gifts; their tastes were just different. He was raised to think a new blender and a box of cherry chocolates made the ideal gift for any woman. It wasn't his fault. Lucky for him that she had seen the potential in his tall, rugged looks and was now refining him into more than his homespun boyhood years had promised.

Robert sneaked up behind her. "Hey, good-lookin'!"

Patricia spun around. "Robert! You scared me!"

He gave her a little squeeze, "You're so cute that I couldn't resist. Sorry for being late. My meeting ran late again."

"I figured as much. That's why I made the twelve-thirty

reservation you suggested for one o'clock." She flashed him
an all-knowing smile.

They were seated at their favorite table in the far corner.
Patricia loved to walk through a restaurant, well aware of the
appreciative glances her beauty drew. Beyond that she required privacy while eating and certainly didn't watch others.

Before looking in the menu, Robert leaned across the
table and asked, "So tell me, since you know me so well,
what do I want for lunch today?"

"Sweet and sour pork, deep-fried shrimp and an egg roll,"
she answered, confidently.

"Close, but no cigar."

"What? That's what you always have!"

"And you always have chicken almondine and jasmine tea."

"I didn't think you'd noticed."

"Ah, yes, you'd be surprised how many things I notice. So
tell me, where are we going to shop ... I mean, look at
decorations today?"

Taken aback, Patricia asked, coyly, "What makes you
think we *will?*"

"I figured as much," he said, flashing her an all-knowing smile.

The cozy little lunch went well. It wasn't until later that
things got out of hand.

Outside Bachman's Robert stopped to place a ten-dollar
bill in the bucket of the Hope For Life bell ringer.

"Why do you always do that?" she whispered loudly, her
gloved hand discreetly half-covering her mouth.

"Because I *can,*" he said matter-of-factly, mimicking
her gesture.

She was not amused. Still, all would have been fine if she
had kept her thoughts to herself as they walked into the
store. "I can't imagine anyone wanting to stand there all
day, ringing a silly bell, collecting money to feed a bunch
of drunks."

Robert stopped in his tracks. Several seconds went by.
Twice he looked as if he was ready to say something
profound. Instead he shook his head. "No, I don't imagine that it would make any sense to you. But I admire
those people."

"It doesn't do any good. People pass them by. No one but you gives more than pocket change."

"Every dollar means a dinner, and giving to them is a Watterson family tradition. You know that."

Oh, ugghh! She was sorry she had mentioned it. It bothered her that Rob felt the need to defend those people, but when he invoked the *Watterson family tradition* it irked her even more. "Anybody can stand and ring a bell. It doesn't take too much talent!"

"Could you?"

"Of course, I could. I just wouldn't want to," she answered with an insincere grin and a mock flutter of her eyelashes, her customary signal to him that the conversation should end. It worked.

They changed the subject, and began the decoration admiration walk, which was not difficult to do because the decorations were truly admirable. Rumor had it that a specialist had been expressly flown in from New York City to bring in the latest ideas in holiday décor. It certainly looked like they'd gotten their money's worth.

It wasn't unusual for people to come in just to ogle the glorious surroundings. It was also quite common for shoppers to buy an inexpensive item: a scarf, a pair of stockings, a box of thin mints, or a gigantic lollipop, simply to get a Bachman's merchandise bag or better yet, an imprinted gift box so that less expensive purchases from other stores could be given a more impressive air.

Not Patricia! This was her store, her favorite place in all of shopping-dom. She was such a regular patroness that many clerks knew her by name, for better or for worse, depending upon her mood of the day. Sharing the splendor of the shopping season with her husband made her absolutely euphoric, so much so that she noticed nothing amiss. Rob was just less talkative than normal.

They talked about additional presents they might buy for their two children, Thomas and Tiffany, and whether to get his secretary a gift certificate or a hand-painted porcelain vase. Then they stopped by the women's department to purchase gloves for his mother. Eventually, "just for fun," they stopped at the most elaborately decorated department

of the entire store, formal wear and furs. Once there
Patricia tried on the fabulous blue fox jacket.

"What do you think?" cooed the triple Patricias perfectly
posed in the full- length, three-way mirror that was el-
egantly draped with an enormous gold-edged, red velvet
bow and tiny white lights.

"I think it looks like bankruptcy for Santa!"

"It does not, silly! I know we can't get it," she reas-
sured him, sensuously running her hand down the
sleeve for another luxurious feel. "I just wondered how
it looks."

Robert studied this alluring blue-eyed creature he had
married and couldn't help softening his attitude. She could
make a gunnysack look good. Incredibly beautiful woman,
but she could be so narrow-minded! Sometimes it was
more than he could stand. At other times, who could resist
her? He stepped up beside her, wrapped his long arms
around her and said, "It looks great, honey."

With exaggerated care Patricia re-hung the fur and
walked away as charmingly and meekly as possible, her
heart racing with expectation. Yes, Patricia thought, the
afternoon had gone well, very well indeed. That was,
of course, until Robert walked her to her car in the
parking plaza.

He was loading their purchases into the trunk when he
stopped, half-lowered the trunk lid, and said, with a mischievous smirk on his face, "I know a way that you could
get that jacket."

"How?"

"You could win it."

"Win it?"

"Yes. In a bet."

Patricia was cool. "I don't bet!"

"Okay," Robert said, letting the topic drop, and closed
the trunk.

Unfortunately her curiosity got the better of her and she
had made that fatal inquiry. It was why today she was
wearing his hunting boots with two pairs of thick socks,
three layers of the best old clothes she could find at
Goodwill—washed three times of course—a stocking cap

covering her meticulously coiffed blonde hair, and sporting a woolen scarf long enough to hide her entire face. It was why she was in a part of the county she normally would not be caught dead in, preparing to stand on the sidewalk and ring a stupid bell for four hours. It was all because Robert had offered her a guaranteed way to win the fur jacket of her dreams, and like a fool, she had asked, "What exactly did you have in mind?"

Mayville, 4:18 p.m.

"All set," Robert said, as he got back into the car.

Patricia gave him one last dismayed look. How she wished he'd say, "You don't need to do this. Or, "It's starting to snow, let's go home."

What he said, as she stepped onto the sidewalk was, "You'll be just fine!" Then he drove off and left her alone.

As Patricia's picture faded, Suzannah's reappeared on the viewer, and the spirit child was delighted. She sat down comfortably on the floor.

Mayville, 4:18 p.m.

Lois, the perfume clerk, eyed Suzannah suspiciously, wondering if she was one of those shoplifting kids planning to take a five-finger discount. If so, this one was not going to get away with it! "Can I help you?" she asked, waiting for the usual, no-I'm-just-looking reply.

However, Suzannah nodded, biting her lower lip. "I don't know what to get," she said shrugging. "I want to get some perfume for my mom, but it sort of costs a lot, doesn't it?"

"Sure does. How much did you want to spend?"

Suzannah hesitated, pulled a little leather coin purse out of her pocket and began re-counting her money. She had secretly hoped that she'd been wrong about the seven dollars and eighty-eight cents, and that if she counted it again there would actually be more than that in her purse. Yet she knew there wasn't. For a minute she even wished she had taken Mom's three dollars. But no, she could manage this.

Now comes the stalling, Lois thought. The kid hasn't got enough. She'll string me along looking at stuff, and when I turn my back she'll grab it and run. Lois was sure of it, clear to the darkened roots of her over-processed red hair, and she started planning the chase.

The hostile-looking clerk made Suzannah even more nervous. "Can I get any for under five dollars?" she asked timidly, her confidence tested. "You see, I gotta get something for my dad too."

Lois was caught off guard. She brusquely explained, "The new kinds cost a lot more than that. Down at the clearance corner you may find something."

"Thanks." Suzannah smiled shyly.

The last of the less popular brands or the watered-down imitations were at the end of the cosmetics display. Suzannah began selectively smelling. Some weren't bad. Some were yucky! Tabu? Tigress? These were okay, but definitely not the kind Mom would wear. She glanced down at the little pink Timex watch Grandpa Brown had sent for her birthday. Twenty-two minutes left. She'd have to smell faster!

From a distance Lois watched the youngster's face change into various grimaces with each sniff. The clerk could appreciate such determination. "This is a serious customer," Lois's Merry-Christmas side told her cynical bah-humbug side, "Come on, give the kid a break!"

That was when she caught sight of the returned merchandise from the day before. A buddy of Mr. Denton's had bought perfume for his wife's birthday, completely forgetting she preferred Avon fragrances, so he was forced to return it. The cute little holiday box it had come in was gone but Mr. Wally said to take it back anyway, that they'd put it on clearance after Christmas. At that point it would be marked down considerably, Lois reasoned, so why not sell it now? This kid obviously needed help, and she, Lois, needed all the sales she could get in order to have a shot at being Salesclerk of the Month, and beat out teenager Tonya for the quarter-an-hour raise. Okay, now she was convinced. "Have you ever heard about Wind Song? You know, the one that says, 'I can't seem to forget you, your Wind Song stays on my mind'?"

Suzannah nodded, her brown eyes brightening with hope.

Lois continued. "It just so happens that I have one bottle left that I could give you a good deal on. It doesn't have the box, but you could wrap it up real cute. Interested?"

"How much?" Suzannah winced, expecting that it still would be too pricey for her meager budget.

"Five dollars. Can you manage that?"

"That would be wonderful!" Suzannah gushed. Her mind's rational side asked, "What in the world can you get for Dad with the rest?" It made her hesitate. "Can you give me a few minutes? I gotta see what I can find for my dad first, then I'll know for sure. Okay?"

Looking into that kid's sweet, eager face, Lois couldn't say no. "Sure, honey. But I go on a coffee break in ten minutes so you'll have to decide by then."

"I will. I will!" Suzannah called over her shoulder and began racing around the store looking for the most perfect $2.88 Christmas present she could find.

The first thing that caught Suzannah's eye was a table covered with several kinds of aftershave. "Maybe this is what I should get," she thought out loud. No, that won't work. Dad wore two kinds of smells. Right Guard deodorant and the shaving cream in the red and white striped can. Other than that, he didn't like to bother with it. Besides, as unhappy as he'd been lately he'd probably say, "Great! Now I stink too!" Suzannah moved down another aisle. Seven minutes left. Hurry, hurry!

Next came a display of work gloves. These might be just the … No! If Dad saw work gloves, he'd probably say, "Well, now I've got work gloves, it's too bad I don't have work!"

He had lost his sense of humor. He wasn't even any good at faking happy either. Last Sunday at church someone had asked him how he was, and instead of saying, "Fine," like everyone does even when they aren't, he actually said, "Not good at all!" Then he stood there and told how bad things were going. She had never been so embarrassed in all her life. So, no work gloves! They cost too much anyway.

With five minutes left to go, a younger clerk named Tonya

came over and asked if she could help. Suzannah told her about needing the perfect $2.88 present as fast as possible. Tonya suggested men's white handkerchiefs. A package of three sturdy cotton ones was on sale for $2.50.

Suzannah shook her head. She could not imagine what he'd use them for; not that he was a slob or anything like that. She couldn't remember *how* he blew his nose, or even *if* he did. Maybe he was a sniff-back spitter like Grandpa. What a drag to realize you don't know such an important detail about your own father! "I don't think so," she said.

"Cherry chocolates! Everybody loves cherry chocolates. And there's a two-pound box on sale, only $1.98!"

"He's allergic to cherries," Suzannah said, shoulders sagging.

"Ok, you keep looking. I've got to help in cosmetics."

"Aaaa!" Suzannah panicked, realizing that her time was up. She grabbed a package of the sturdy, white cotton hankies and raced across the store to the cosmetics counter, dodging other customers along the way.

Lois was more than happy to ring up Suzannah's purchases. Tonya seemed rather surprised to see the girl at the cosmetics counter when she arrived, and getting such a fantastic deal on the perfume. Not to be outdone, she came up with a brilliant idea and a jewelry gift box into which the perfume bottle fit perfectly. "It might be best to put the hankies in a bag by themselves and hide the perfume safely in your deepest pocket," she suggested, tucking another flattened gift box into Suzannah's bag, with a wink. "Then if your Mom gets curious, she'll only the see the hankies."

"Thank you so much. Merry Christmas!" Suzannah gushed, and all but skipped to the front of the store.

<hr />

A picture of a man driving a pickup truck appeared.

Ginny looked surprised. "For goodness sakes, it's Harvey Watterson. Oh... so it's that Patricia! I thought the couple in the car looked a bit familiar."

"Is that her father? He looks nice."

"No, he's Patricia's father-in-law, and yes, he's a very nice man, a true friend."

"Is he connected to my family too?"
"If Patricia is, he is. This should be interesting."

***

Hometown, 4:20 p.m.

Harvey Watterson pulled out of his yard in the old Chevy 4-by-4 pickup he called "Old Blue" when no one was around. No amount of snow was going to keep him home! He felt like going to town and by heck, he was a'goin'!

He didn't feel like helping with the old folks' Christmas bash at the Hometown Legion Hall. Just after Thanksgiving they'd asked someone else to play Santa in the Hometown Holiday Parade again and yes, it still irked him, so he'd stayed home and been bored all afternoon. But he'd taken his fill of boredom right fast and made the excuse that he needed to run into Mayville to pick up the dry cleaning and get a box of Polident.

Of course his wife had seen through it all, but she hadn't tried to stop him. Enid knew his truck could practically climb a telephone pole; so a little snow didn't worry her. She needed more walnuts, powdered sugar, and colored sprinkles in order to finish her Christmas baking anyway, and gladly added those items to his list. Besides, she was tired of his pacing around the house grumbling about what he *ought* to be doing.

Enid understands, he thought, as he turned onto Estates Lane. Half a mile down the road he passed Riverwood Estates.

Riverwood! It was a highly creative name that had nothing to do with reality. The closest thing to a river nearby was an irrigation canal and the closest thing to a forest that hadn't been ripped out for field planting years ago was the big evergreens by his house, and a row of saplings he'd planted as a windbreak for the garden. Be that as it may, Riverwood had made a big impact on the area and on his life.

Who could have imagined that it would come to this? Nobody. Not even Harve himself. Fifteen years ago, when he received a small, unexpected inheritance, Harvey had bought a thousand acres of unproductive hay fields. They were called "the flats" then, and when he moved his family west of Mayville onto the old farm on the edge of

Hometown, people had laughed. It was the "Seward's Folly" of Wadimoor County, and he was nicknamed Hare-Brained Harvey. Nobody had a clue that within ten years the area would be *the* place to live in the valley. Or that when the freeway went through so many city-ites would head out that way, turning Hometown into what they now called an up-and-coming bedroom community.

Harvey drove past the subdivision entrance with its name elaborately inscribed on bronze-colored aluminum on a 2-by-6-foot brick wall, illuminated every night by a couple of 4-inch floodlights. It all seemed mighty pretentious to his way of thinking. But the buyers had come in droves. Sixty one-third-acre lots were sold in no time. It was downright amazing! Then again so was the fact that some folks called him Mr. Watterson now instead of Harvey, and began treating him like he was supposed to know more because he had money for the first time in his life. It had been an ego boost at first, yet had caused him grief, too.

Years ago the Town Council had asked him to be the clown in the parade for the 4th of July celebration. He'd collect candy donations from Bud's Bargain-All and Home-town Foodmart, and gum from Heber's Hardware and had a great time handing it out to the little kids, and teasing the teenage girls to trade candy for a kiss. The girls always shied away from his thickly painted mug, and the little kids laughed. There was never enough candy to go around 'cause the adults begged for a few pieces too.

Exhausted and thoroughly melted by the time the parade was over, he'd wash up and head back to Hometown Park to help the Lions Club sell hot dogs and hamburgers, drive the tractor for the bumpy trailer ride or emcee the patriotic talent show.

For seven years he'd also played Santa Claus in the parade and for the Hometown Holiday shindig that they held down at Town Hall afterwards. He was proud to be a part of that and always listened intently to the wishes of kids from miles around. He'd been a Boy Scout leader for twelve years and seen a whole generation grow up and get on with their lives. It was gratifying.

"Mr. Watterson" didn't get asked to do these things, as if

people thought he'd find it undignified, or assumed he was too busy. He was barely sixty—okay, sixty-three—tall, robust. He had worked his tail off every day to support his family and keep the wolf away from the door and always thought he'd be happier rich. Now that he had money and time on his hands he knew that wasn't true. Harvey shook his head sadly. Fancy shmancy Riverwood!

It hadn't been his idea to name it that. It was all his daughter-in-law Patricia's idea. She'd said their subdivision should have an upper-class image if they expected to draw upper-class builders for upper-class buyers. His son, Harvey Robert, whose idea it had been to develop the land, didn't argue with her. No sir, when it came to upper-class things, Patricia Eagler Watterson was an expert!

She had lived on the wealthy side of The City all her life and when Harvey Robert married her that's exactly where they went, four blocks away from her parents in a new-fangled upper-class thing called a condominium. Now his country-raised kid who had been called Harve Bob or Bobby most of his life was a city-ite calling himself H. Robert Watterson of Watterson Developments, Inc. And although many referred to Harvey as Mr. Watterson, he was still the clown from the county to his daughter-in-law. She would smile and obligingly turn her cheek for him to kiss whenever they came to visit. Harvey didn't dislike Patricia. She was pretty, and was a basically decent person yet it was plain that she had little use for him.

Certainly she couldn't find fault with Enid. Why, the woman was a saint! Besides that, she was remarkable. She could feed twenty people at the drop of a hat, and had won so many ribbons for baked goods at the Wadimoor County Fair that they had made her a judge in that division just so other people could have a chance to win for a change. She was often asked to speak at church and used to play the organ each Sunday until her arthritis kicked in. Then there was her garden and the rows of home-canned goods that lined the shelves of their basement cellar. Yes, Enid was a wonder! Soft-spoken, yet gracious enough to make anyone he brought home feel welcome. Sure, she was a bit plumper than she'd like to be, but she cleaned up real nice. Not like him, big and loud and lacking in refinement. As far as he could tell, this was what irked his daughter-in-law the most.

True that he was no fashion plate either. His favorite everyday outfit was a pair of bib overalls, plaid shirt and tan Carhart jacket. These were generally new looking or at least clean and in good repair. Enid always saw to that. And when he went into The City on business to sign papers at the bank he always wore a nice navy blue suit and his pride and joy; a custom-made black ten-gallon cowboy hat. He figured that if it was good enough for Hoss Cartwright, it was good enough for him, so Patricia's opinion didn't worry him. He was himself, for better or worse.

It did goad him, though, that Patricia had been right about Riverwood, and that she didn't trust him to name it something sensible, as though he'd call it Watterson's Pit or Harvey's Hole-in-the-Ground. No, she'd had her way naming that one. But he'd insisted that *his* wife have some consideration too, so in the middle of the ritzy homes there was a nice little cul-de-sac called Enid Gate.

They'd be selling lots in subdivision number two next spring. Rivercrest. Patricia again! Subdivision three was already on the drawing board. It would be the one closest to his house, and by George, he wanted it filled with regular homes and regular people! He'd already decided to call it *Rosewood*, because Rose was Enid's middle name, and instead of flood-lights, there'd be rosebushes. So there, Patricia!

His truck slid at the stop sign as he slowed to turn. "Whoa, Blue," he said out loud, as if his truck had gears *and* ears. "Better slow down." He turned left onto Wood-land Road for the drive to Mayville.

───※───

Suzannah's picture reappeared on the screen. The spirit child clapped with delight.

───※───
Mayville, 4:50 p.m.
Thank goodness Mom is always late for things, Suzannah mused. She was tickled to pieces about her purchases, and

rushed to greet her mother, who was standing next to a ladies' glove display.

"What do you think?" Carol asked, holding up a purple-gloved right hand and a red-gloved left hand, when Suzannah reached her side

"I like the purple ones better. They match your coat."

"I know, but the red ones feel the best."

"Then get the red ones. They match *my* coat."

"If I decide to buy gloves, it'll be so I can get to work without frozen fingers, not so you can build better snowmen!"

"We'll see!"

Carol gave Suzannah's nose a playful purple tweak then handed her a tiny bag of warm cashews. "If I let you hold these while I check out will there be any left?"

"Only if you hurry!" Suzannah teased her mother again.

⚊⚊⚊⚊⚊

The focus of the screen turned to another young woman. Her feet barely kept her steady as she maneuvered along the icy sidewalk to the Mayville drugstore.

"Another one? Who is this?" The spirit child stood up whining. Ginny answered with a shrug and a smile.

⚊⚊⚊⚊⚊

Mayville, 4:57 p.m.

How Maria hated snow! It crowded around her ankles and fell into her shoes as she walked. Summer shoes! She had not planned on being here once the snow came; now her feet stung from the cold. She scolded herself for not accepting Jean Martin's offer to buy her some boots and a warmer coat. Pride! Such foolish pride! But by taking them she would have been admitting that she had to stay here, and she would not, could not do that. Eduardo will come for me soon, she kept telling herself. Somehow he will find me. Then we will leave this wintry place and go home.

It had been four months since she had last heard from her husband. In the meantime, she stayed with Jean, a kind, older woman she had met when her little Carlos was in the hospital. She liked Jean, but she did not like snow, or the wind that bit through the old gray poplin coat that she clutched tightly around herself. She kept walking.

Mayville, 5:09 p.m.

Suzannah and her mom left the Five and Dime bombarded by snow that made the sidewalks as treacherous as the streets. "Mom, can we drop a dollar into that bell ringer's bucket? She looks *so* sad," Suzannah asked.

"How can you tell? Her face is all covered up!"

"Well, I'd be sad if I had to do that. It's awful cold. Can't we give her something, *please?*"

Carol felt a twinge of guilt. She had passed by the bell-ringing woman earlier for two reasons. First, she'd seen the type of car the woman had gotten out of, and it wasn't exactly a poverty-mobile. Secondly, money was too scarce to give away this year. Still Suz hadn't taken the three dollars she'd been offered earlier, so why not? "Okay," she gave in.

Suzannah walked back to drop in her money. A tall, older man came up about the same time and placed a ten-dollar bill in the pot.

"It isn't much," Suzannah apologized, holding out the dollar.

"Every dollar's a dinner," the man said. The bell-ringing lady made an odd, whimpering-puppy kind of noise.

"Merry Christmas," Suzannah called over her shoulder as she hurried to catch up to her mom.

"Merry Christmas," boomed the nice, older man in a great jolly voice that reminded Suzannah of the neat Santa that they used to have at the Hometown holiday bash. It wasn't as realistic when they replaced him with a shorter guy who had to stuff a pillow in his suit.

I'm too old for that stuff now anyway, she thought.

Mayville, 5:12 p.m.

On the last stretch of sidewalk before the parking lot Suzannah and her mom began sliding, and giggling. Maria rounded the corner moments later. A friendly collision ensued. Trying not to knock Maria down, Suzannah caught her balance and dodged right. All three slipped, nearly falling several times, helping to steady one second or needing help to be steadied the next. Finally Suzannah maneuvered around Maria safely. Carol followed tiptoeing. "I'm *so* sorry. Merry Christmas!" she nodded and smiled as she passed.

Maria absorbed their laughter as they continued slip-sliding to their car. She thought of her own mother. Home-sickness engulfed her. She was desperate to go home, but her return was forbidden. Now in this icy hell, she missed her husband, her mother, and the comfort of family. She pulled the coat closely around her middle again, as if to give extra warmth to the tiny one growing within.

Eduardo didn't know she was expecting again, nor did her mother, who had attended her when Carlos was born. Anguish welled her throat. She wondered who would attend her when *this* baby came, now that she had no home?

The bitter wind assailed her ankles, bringing her quickly back to the present. She turned again toward the medicine store and nearly tripped over a white paper bag. Picking it up, she began to wave. "Señora! Señorita!" she called.

It was too late. The mother and daughter were pulling away in their car and did not hear her.

<hr />

Mayville, 5:18 p.m.
The next picture was that of a short, sharp-faced, balding man. He paced nervously up and down by the front window of his drugstore, becoming increasingly irritated at the onslaught of snow.

Ginny gasped.

"What is it?"

Ginny winked at the spirit child. "You'll see," was all she would say.

<hr />

Del Jones was not having a good day. He wondered how the heck he would get home. He had left his car at Moyd's Motors that morning so they could find the leak in the radiator and someone from there had dropped him off at work. Around 4 p.m. their office gal had called to say that his car wouldn't be ready until Monday. He was stranded and annoyed. Normally he would have walked the five blocks home, but in this weather? Mentally he wasn't wishing good old Mr. Moyd a Merry Christmas.

To his customers, Del was very professional as he walked around the pleasantly decorated, neatly-shelved store helping whomever wherever with whatever was needed. He handed out sympathy or candy canes as efficiently as he did the pills and powders from the pharmacy counter. Many people were having a rough time, and listening to their confidences had left him feeling drained.

Inwardly he was a defeated man, himself. He tried not to add to anyone's misery or ruin the Christmas spirit by being ill-tempered, but he was not by nature a social creature. It had taken great self-control, but he hadn't bitten anyone's head off ... yet. So far he'd fought the urge to stand in the center of the store and yell, "Go home!" so he could, too. The last thing he needed was another problem.

Maria approached meekly. He knew she was staying with Jean Martin and often came in with a note explaining what was needed. But tonight when Maria handed him Jean's note, he was suddenly swamped in a sea of Spanish with only a shaky "Yo no hablo Español," to keep him afloat.

Maria had hoped that Del would tell her what to do with the package the little girl had dropped. She wanted to return it to its rightful owner. Unfortunately Del didn't speak Spanish and Maria didn't know enough English to explain herself. Soon both became frustrated.

"Harvey! Thank goodness! Hey, come over here a minute," Del hollered across the store, as soon as he saw his longtime pal come through the door. "Boy, am I glad to see you!"

"What's up, Del? Shoplifters?" Harvey asked.

"Shoplifters? Where?" Del scrambled to the second of two steps that led up to the pharmacy prescription booth and began peering in all directions.

"How would I know? You brought up shoplifters. You tell me."

"No, you did! Boy did you ever jump to conclusions."

"Not as fast as you jumped up those steps. Man, are you

skittish today!" Harvey said with a big grin. "So what do you need then?"

Skittish? Del growled inwardly. His voice betrayed his irritation. "This young lady has been trying to tell me something and I'll be darned if I can make heads or tails of it. Please talk to her and figure it out before I lose my mind and what's left of my hair."

"Sure." Harvey turned calmly to Maria with a manner that reminded her of her kindly, quirky grandfather. "¿Cuál es el problema?"

"Encontré este paquete en la nieve, se le callo a una niña, y no se como regresarselo. Podria usted llevarselo?"

"What'd she say?" Del Jones asked, eagerly.

Harvey turned and explained, "Seems that she's found this bag and wants you to find its owner."

"How the heck am I supposed to know who ...? It's a Five and Dime bag, not one of mine." Then curiosity caught hold of Del and he asked, "What's in it?"

Harvey turned to Maria again. "¿Que hay en el paquete?"

Maria shrugged and handed it to him. Harvey turned away from them and peeked into it.

"Ah-hah!" he said, acting mysteriously. "This is serious business, Del. You sure you wanna know?"

Del Jones looked worried. Maria watched with guarded interest. With their full attention, Harvey slowly reached into the bag. Without warning he yelled, "It's got me! It's got me!"" And shook his arm around in the bag.

Del rushed forward in one second, in the next he ducked backward as "it" flew at him, striking him on the chin. "Aaah," he yelled, lashing out with his arm to protect himself, knocking the package of hankies senseless to the floor. A sidesplitting guffaw erupted from Harvey. He leaned against the prescription counter for support.

Startled, Maria soon began to giggle, then covered her mouth to respectfully suppress it. Yes, this kind, quirky man *was* like her grandfather, she thought, un poco loco!

Indignation clouded Del's face. Luckily, he was able to shake it before any caustic comments flew out of his mouth, but he was not amused. "Dang it, Harvey! You scared the wits out of me!"

"Sorry, Del. Didn't know you were so afraid of hankies."

"I couldn't tell *what* was flying at my face, and since it's the only face I've got, I figured I'd protect it," Del picked up the package and tried to brush off the traces of the stomp mark left by his size 8 Hush Puppies. He examined it carefully, shaking his head. "Better tell her that there's no way of knowing who they belong to. See if she wants them."

Harvey explained to Maria that the owner could not be found and told her to take the package home.

"Gracias," she nodded to both men as she left with the hankies and Jean's medicine.

"No hay problema! "Harvey answered, sincerely.

Not to be outdone again, Del nodded, "Adios!"

Neither man could help noticing how Maria lingered in the toy aisles, longingly gazing at all the displays on her way out of the store.

"D'ya know her?" Harvey asked, when she was finally gone.

"Yeah, a bit. She's got quite a story. Be glad to tell ya if you stick around for a while and give me a lift home. Car's in the garage."

"No hay problema! Gonna grab some hot chocolate and run a couple of errands. Back in a bit."

As Harvey headed for the soda fountain, Del called out, "You scared me to death, ya loony old coot!"

Harvey shook his head and burst out laughing again. "Oh, the look on your face! It must have been like the look on *my* face last November at the sunrise service, when I tried to play Taps and found someone had soaped the mouthpiece of my bugle. Eh, Del?"

"Ya got no proof it was me, Harve."

"Some things ya just know, Del. Some things ya just know!"

Mayville, 5:45 p.m.

An assaulting gust of wind whipped through Maria's thin coat again as she left the store. Crystallized snow nipped at her ankles. Her hatred of winter weather was rapidly rekindled.

Eduardo, Eduardo! She called to her husband in her mind, as if searching for him there would bring a sense of needed warmth. The sting of tears could have easily over-whelmed her had she not heard a mournful sound as she passed the woman with the bell. Maria suddenly stopped.

"Why is Maria standing there?" the little spirit inquired.

"Someone just sent her a message. It's permitted some-times, in special cases." Ginny said, indicating the screen next to them where a man stood looking at the same picture of Maria as they were. She recognized him as the escort of her last little friend.

The spirit child approached him. "Maria's your girl?"

He nodded pleasantly.

The child held out her hand. "She's part of our Christmas connection. We should watch together!"

He took her right hand with his left, placed his right hand against the shimmering light and repeated, "Tu corazón no es el único que llora." Your heart is not the only one that cries.

Maria opened the package of hankies, separated one from the rest, and returned to give it to the bell woman. "Feliz Navidad," she said, softly, then hurried back to Jean's as carefully as possible.

Mayville, 7:12 p.m.

Robert returned earlier than planned, concerned about the storm, and certain that Patricia would have had enough by now. When he pulled up to the curb in front of her, she stood there, debating whether to get into his car or kick it. Robert got out to open the door for her, then gathered up the bell stand and collection pot.

"How'd it go? You feel okay?" he asked, when they got settled in the car.

Patricia did not answer. She simply proceeded to unwrap her face so that she could glare at him properly. How did it go? How did she feel? The questions raced through her indignant mind like a blazing trail of ignited dominoes. It was the only warm spot on her body. The rest was substantially frozen, thank you.

Robert didn't push for an answer. He could tell she needed time to sort things out.

"Mom sent some hot chocolate and fresh-baked cookies," he offered cheerfully after they'd driven a couple of miles.

Patricia was aghast. "You told your mother?"

"Yes. I had to. How else could I explain why I surprised her with an unexpected three hour-visit, by myself?"

"You told your mother!" Patricia shrieked, shaking her head, incredulously. Now she was humiliated *and* mad.

"Don't worry. Mom won't tell a soul, not even Dad. I told her you were doing it as a kind of service project. She thought it was an incredibly sweet thing to do."

"That does it! I cannot get away from your family, no matter how hard I try."

"What's that supposed to mean?"

"Nothing," Patricia said flatly, giving him her phony half-smile and quick flutter of eyelashes.

"You can't say that and expect me to drop it. Exactly what did you mean?" he inquired, sitting at attention. His neck turned stiffly, checking the rearview mirror and the side mirror twice, then he stared out the windshield. Patricia referred to this as his "destination animation," in which he acted as though he were in total driving concentration when he was very ticked off. It was time to explain herself.

"All right, all right," she said. "What I meant was … Well, actually, I don't know what I meant. It's just that I was so nervous all afternoon; afraid someone would recognize me. Then who shows up? Your dad!"

"Mom said she'd sent him to Mayville. He was antsy and driving her crazy," Robert said, with a slight smile.

"That's it. He was driving me crazy too!"

"You mean he recognized you?"

"No, not exactly. I don't think he did."

"Then what?"

"He kept coming to see me. First it was to put some money into the tub, bucket, whatever it's called. He came back later to talk and brought hot chocolate and a donut from the drugstore."

"Did you eat it?" Robert asked, trying not to smirk.

"I had to! There was nowhere to put it. He stood there talking while I did."

Robert grinned thinking, that's my dad! He continued calmly, "Anything else?"

"He got really *personal*, asked all sorts of questions. I had to keep my face covered, except for a small opening, and talk in a squeaky way so he wouldn't recognize my voice."

"Personal questions?"

"Very personal."

"What did he say?" Robert asked, worried.

"If you must know, he said that if I needed a break, you know, to use the restroom or anything, that he'd be glad to ring the bell and guard the money."

"That *is* personal," Robert said, trying to keep a straight face. "Did he actually use the word restroom?"

"No. But I knew that's what he meant." Patricia darted an analytical look his way, trying to determine if his last comment was sincere or sarcastic. If it were sarcasm, the conversation would be over.

Robert rapidly donned his most sincere look. "Then what happened?" he urged, carefully.

Patricia sighed. "When I came back, he started asking questions like, was I ready for Christmas, did I have any kids, what did they want for Christmas, that sort of thing. I couldn't risk him recognizing me, so I made up a story about how my son was a bit hyper, but friendly, and my daughter was an artistic chatterbox."

"Wouldn't that be nice," Robert muttered under his breath.

"What? There is nothing wrong with our children!"

"I know, I know. It's just that they are so shy. It would be nice if they were a little more outgoing, wouldn't it?"

"I suppose," Patricia agreed, guardedly.

"So what about the presents? Did he give you those too?"

Patricia nodded. "I'll give them to the Center, in case a little kid happens to show up sometime. It's probably not stuff our kids would like." She hurriedly continued with her story before Robert could add further comment. "After that, Harvey went away for a while. Then a bizarre thing happened. It was so strange, and I was miserably cold … I might have imagined it."

"Sounds serious. What happened?"

"I don't know if I can talk about it. Promise you won't have me locked up?"

"Don't worry."

"Okay, but don't forget your promise!"

She told about feeling dejected, mortified, and numb. Harvey wasn't there to bug her anymore, but no one else was stopping to give money either. She admitted developing a pitiful case of sniffles. "I hadn't seen anyone for quite a while. Just stood there, staring at my boots. The next thing I knew, there was a pretty young Mexican woman standing next to me. She had on an old-fashioned summer coat that was practically falling apart, hardly anything in the way of shoes and this itty-bitty scarf to keep the snow off her head. This poor lady smiled so sweetly and handed me a large white handkerchief. Then she said Merry Christmas in Spanish, I think."

"I could see where that might seem strange."

"No! You don't understand," Patricia said, through re-newed tears. "Here I was, bundled up from head to toe, blubbering away out on the sidewalk, and this woman came to comfort *me!* I was very touched. I took the hand-kerchief and turned away so she wouldn't see me blow my nose, of course."

"Of course."

"When I turned back to thank her, she was gone. It was like she vanished! I looked, but couldn't see her anywhere. People began leaving stores quickly and the snow came down like crazy. I thought about how the lady looked and what she'd done, and felt like I had been visited by ... by an angel, or something."

"An angel?"

"I know, it's ridiculous!" Patricia took a big, white hankie out of her coat pocket and turned away to blow her nose.

Robert was tempted to hum the Twilight Zone theme song. Her humility made him think twice. "Well, I'm glad someone was looking out for you." Robert patted her knee, relieved that the experience hadn't been a complete disas-ter. A moment later he added, "The roads are awfully bad, should we stop at the Center to drop off the money to-night, or wait until Monday?"

Patricia wiped her nose again and sat up straight. "Let's do it tonight. I've got some shopping to do on Monday. Don't I?" She fluttered her eyelashes and smiled.

Mayville, 8:19 p.m.

"Truck's over there," Harvey called out, pointing across the street to the front of the dry cleaner's. Del finished locking the drugstore, then hurried after him.

Both men stomped snow off their boots before closing the truck doors, but it fell in such flurries, it was hard to tell which let in the most, the boots or the open doors.

Harvey had to step out again to loosen the icebound windshield wipers. "Brrrr," he said, as he got back in and turned on defrost. "My bones are getting too old for this."

"Sure know what you mean there. Makes me feel even worse when I think about that little Mexican gal running around in those shabby shoes."

"Who is she, anyway?"

"Name's Maria Sanchez. She's staying with Jean Martin, you know, couple of blocks down, corner of Ash and Oak."

Harvey nodded. Since the move to Hometown years ago, he hadn't seen the Martins much, but knew of them. Jean's husband, Art had been active in the American Legion before he died of prostate trouble about three years back.

Del continued, "Jean does volunteer work at Children's Hospital. That's where she met Maria. She and her husband are migrant workers. Anyway, their little boy's almost three. During this past picking season he got terribly sick and ended up needing a heart valve or something."

"Good grief! How'd they pay for that?"

"March of Dimes covered it, I think. And it's a good thing, because the little guy had to stay in the hospital for a long time to recover. In the meantime, Maria's husband had to head out for the winter job he had lined up in California or Arizona somewhere. Now the boy's better but they've lost track of each other. Jean's taking care of them until the husband's found."

"That Jean is sure a kind soul," Harvey said, driving the

truck back and forth a couple of times to get traction before pulling onto the road.

"Yup. I guess that Spanish came in handy after all."

"What?"

"Thought I'd told you about her giving Virginia the Spanish lessons?"

"Don't think you did."

Del paused. "Jean and Virginia had a lot of time on their hands, and Virginia needed to concentrate on something, you know, besides ... the pain. So Jean decided to teach her some Spanish."

"Didn't realize that."

"Yeah." Del nodded. "Nutty idea in some ways, if you think about it, but it seemed to help and they had fun with it. Jean had learned a bunch from helping her girl study in junior high and high school."

Del became quiet once more.

Harvey knew Jean Martin had helped out a lot when Del's Virginia was sick.

They knew each other from the Relief Society at church and had become very close during the illness. He'd seen a photo of them wearing matching headscarves that Jean made when Virginia lost her hair. He knew how grateful Del must be, but could only imagine what else his buddy was feeling. Enid said they should keep track of Del this Christmas, since it would be his first one alone.

"Del's a brick. He'll tough it out," he'd told her. Enid had known better. Now Harvey could see it too. The silence was uncomfortable. He tried to get Del talking again. "I learned Spanish years ago, what little I know. There was a guy in my barracks from New Mexico."

"Sorry. What'd you say?"

"Never mind," Harvey said, as he drove up in front of Del's dark, lonely house and left the motor running, in case Del wanted to talk some more.

Del sat staring toward the front door. After a minute he said, "Just when you think they can't take anymore, the pain gets worse. I couldn't stand it. I'd make an excuse to go check on the store. Jean was a lot stronger that way. She gladly came over."

Harvey rested his right hand on Del's shoulder. "Don't be hard on yourself. You were wonderful with Virginia. She told Enid so."

"Really?"

"Sure. You know she was crazy about ya, you rascal!"

Del grinned. "Well, better let you go. I'll bet Enid's wondering where you got lost to. Thanks again for all you did tonight."

"Anytime, buddy. Anytime at all." Harvey cleared his own throat. Then changing the subject, he added, "Been thinking about fixing up my old tractor, adding a snow blade. I could take care of my own drive, and swing down to Riverwood. I've got the time, and I don't think the county would mind the help."

"It'd be pretty expensive wouldn't it?" Del asked, glad for the switch in topics.

"Not with the right mechanic."

"For heaven's sake, don't take it to Moyd's."

Both men laughed and took turns telling mechanical horror stories until Del said, "Appreciate the ride. Guess I could've walked."

"Wasn't any kind of imposition. Don't forget, Christmas dinner's at two o'clock."

"I won't. Tell Enid to make lots of pie!"

"You got it. See ya later."

When Harvey saw the hallway light go on he honked once and drove off. He didn't envy Del being alone in that house. Little if anything had been moved out of place since the day Virginia died. One pair of her shoes was still by the door, her clothes in the closet, including a new Christmas coat that she'd never had a chance to wear. Her reading glasses and open turned-over bible were on the seat of the rocking chair as if she had just set them there and would be back any minute. But the Virginia-feel was gone.

The Christmassy things like colored lights lining the gables and threaded through the lilac bushes by the front gate were missing, as was a wreath on the door and the specially lit manger scene that was usually on the porch. There were no tantalizing baking smells or sounds of Virginia practicing hymns on the piano.

Life left the house when Virginia did. No wonder Del dreaded going in there alone, Harvey thought. "Time to get home, Blue!" He revved up the engine and pulled back onto the road, grateful to have someone to go home to.

The spirit child sat on the azure tiled floor, perplexed. "Do you understand it all?" Ginny watched as Del entered his home. She noticed that he turned off the light as soon as Harvey Watterson left and sat in the unlit living room on the arm of the recliner for quite a while before heading into the bedroom.

"Ginny?" the little one tugged on her long blue sleeve, "Ginny!"

"Sorry, child, what did you say?"

"Do you understand what's happening?"

"Not yet. The pieces are coming together, like a puzzle."

"What's a puzzle?"

"It's a toy with a hidden picture that has to be put together one piece at a time. It can be slow going, but is usually worth it in the end."

"I don't think I'll like puzzles."

"I'm not surprised. But don't give up, little one. Each day brings another clue." The luminous screen lit up again.

Sunday, December 19, 1965

San Vega, 6:45 a.m.

Jake Boyer sat up abruptly in bed. His wife, Connie rolled over toward him and rubbed his lower back. "Have that nightmare again?"

Jake nodded, pressing down on his forehead with both palms. "Can't get it out of my mind."

Three-year-old Ronnie wandered into the room sleepy-eyed, hoping to crawl into bed with his parents for a quick snuggle. Connie reached down to pick him up. "Ooh!" she groaned. "You are dripping wet, kiddo. You're not getting in my bed. You're getting into the tub!"

Ronnie ran out of the room giggling.

"Looks like it'll be a while before you can get into the shower." As she put on the matching robe to her lavender nightie, Connie studied the expression on her husband's face. This football-player-sized guy had been tossing and turning in their double bed all night, so she hadn't slept much either. She reached across to his side of the bed and soothingly ran her fingers through his dark, wavy hair. "Try to go back to sleep for a few minutes at least."

From the direction of the bathroom came a mysterious clatter of something being knocked into the tub and a delighted squeal from Ronnie. "He's having too much fun. I'd better get in there."

Jake smiled wearily and lay back down. Asleep or awake, he couldn't get the incident out of his mind. It had been the strangest Saturday of his life. He was ticked off at his younger brother Steve for coming late to the warehouse to help load the truck. Boyer Brothers Inc. was a fledgling produce delivery company and was bound to stay that way unless the two brothers could work out their differences and work as a team. In Jake's opinion, Steve's mind wasn't on the game. He'd turned into a total flake since he'd met that Linda girl.

Not that Jake didn't approve of her; she was okay... for a redhead. Of course she wasn't as great as his Connie; a sassy-looking honey-blonde, not too tall, built real nice and a great little mother, too. Linda was more on the skimpy side figure-wise but not bad and actually pretty nice. What he didn't like about the situation was how distracted and unreliable Steve had become. "Late again? You aren't the only one with a life around here," he'd hollered.

"I'm sorry," Steve had hollered back. "What else do you want?"

"Would it be too much to ask for a little concentration today? We've got things to do. I want to take Connie and Ronnie around to see the Christmas lights tonight."

"Yeah? Well at least you got a wife and a kid to take around!" Steve snarled.

"If that's what you want, marry Linda and get it over with!"

"Yeah right, like I'm supposed to make that kind of a decision based on seeing her one night a week!"

"It's not *that* bad."

"It's not? We load before dawn each Saturday for the short run. We get home late Saturday night. We load again at eight on Sunday morning for the long haul and get back late on Wednesday night, if we're lucky!"

"It won't be like this forever. It takes time to get a business going. You knew that. In the meantime ..."

"In the meantime," Steve interrupted, "I get to drive miles on end wondering if Linda will be glad to see me each Friday, or tell me to get lost." He jerked the truck door open, slammed it shut, turned on the motor and jammed the stick shift, grinding it into gear.

Jake threw his arms up, and bellowed, "Hey, grind a pound for me while you're at it!"

"Be glad to. Where do you want me to put it?" Steve bellowed back.

Jake had been tempted to tell him exactly where to put it, but that would have been too easy. He waved Steve off, "Back up without breaking the dang truck, would ya!"

Once again, Boyer Brothers Deliveries, Inc., had proven to all within earshot how splendidly they could communicate. Neither spoke to the other again until the truck was loaded. Sid, the warehouse manager at Poulson Produce, always had plenty of willing Mexican workers around so loading went fast. Jake didn't know much about these guys. They seemed like an okay bunch; hard workers who weren't paid much. No doubt stingy old Sid cut back on their wages whenever he could. It wasn't the decent thing to do, still it wasn't his problem, Jake told himself.

Jake checked off the last few crates of lemons, grapefruit and oranges.

"I've got five crates of cantaloupe left, if you think you can use 'em," Sid offered.

"Sure," Jake said, reasonably sure that someone along the route would be interested in them.

Within minutes Sid had someone from his crew bring all five crates and stack them onto a hand truck ready for Jake to push onto his truck. Steve, of course, knew nothing about the extra crates of cantaloupes, so when he no longer heard any movement in the back he assumed the loading was finished, adjusted the volume on the radio, and pulled away from the dock. During the same time frame, Jake had begun pushing the heavy stack toward the edge of the 5-foot high dock.

A Mexican guy in a red shirt started yelling and waving his arms like a crazy. Jake couldn't imagine why the guy would be signaling him, so he ignored the man and kept pushing the load. The next thing Jake knew, a red blur knocked him sideways down onto the concrete floor. Immediately Jake pushed the guy off him and scrambled to regain his footing. He staggered, fist clenched ready to wallop his attacker when he heard the crash!

He spun around and stared over the edge of the dock in horror. Pieces of wooden crates went flying every which way. Wounded cantaloupes lay with their guts open to the world. A few lucky ones rolled wildly away, and the hand truck he'd been pushing lay in a twisted heap. A sickening rush of reality hit Jake. How easily he could have fallen over the 5-foot drop and been down there with a broken back, or neck!

Steve jumped out of the truck. "What the heck are you doing up there?"

"You stupid idiot! You almost got me killed! How come ya moved the truck?" He began to tremble.

"I thought you were finished!"

"I almost was, *permanently*, thanks to you! And would have been, if it hadn't been for that little Mexican guy."

"Little Mexican guy? What are you talkin' about? And what's with this mess? Cantaloupes? We didn't order canta-loupes," Steve yelled back, waving his arms in disbelief at the destroyed fruit.

"Never mind about that now. I'll tell ya about the stinkin' fruit later. Listen, while you were driving off there was a guy; one of these worker guys here pushed me out of the way, kept me from going over the edge. He saved my neck!"

"Sorry! How was I supposed to know what you were up to?"

"You could have looked."

"You could have warned me! Anyway, you seem fine. Can we go now?"

"You don't understand. There was this guy ... I gotta find him." With that Jake ran into the warehouse on an urgent quest to find his rescuer. Warehouse workers scattered in his wake. The guy was nowhere to be found.

Steve found his brother searching hopelessly. "Come on, man," he said, awkwardly putting his arm around the big guy's shoulder. "It'll be okay. Let's go. I'm sure Sid will tell him you said thanks."

Jake left reluctantly.

Boyer Bros. Inc. deliveries were unusually late that day. Jake called and talked to Connie for almost an hour around noon. That night the near-disaster replayed in his sleep repeatedly, like a bad movie with no popcorn.

"Maybe it means something," Connie said, after he woke up the second time.

"Means something? What are you talking about, means something?"

"I don't know. Just something," she said, sleepily.

Actually he'd wondered too, just hated to admit it. The whole situation was downright spooky, and dang it, he was no pantywaist! The next idea that popped into his brain was even spookier; very much out of character. He mulled it over for a while, then reached over to pick up the telephone.

"Steve? I was thinking that we could load up later today, say around eleven." There was a pause. "Well, because there's somewhere I gotta go for a couple of hours. It's important." Another pause. "Yeah, I know what I said. Look, I can't explain it right now. I'll see you then, okay? Maybe you can take what's-her-face to breakfast for a change." Then he laughed and said, "If she gets mad about an early call from the guy she supposedly loves, it ought to tell you something. Good luck. See ya later."

"What was that all about?" Connie asked, as she came returned from the bathroom carrying a towel-wrapped Ronnie.

Jake was embarrassed. "If I tell ya, you'll think I'm nuts."

She smiled. "Won't be the first time, so what can it hurt?" Ronnie wriggled from her arms and began bouncing on the bed in the buff.

Ginny quickly covered the spirit child's eyes.

"Okay, don't faint. I sort of feel like going to church."

Connie's mouth fell open. Then her eyes narrowed slightly, "Don't mess with me, Jake. It's not funny."

"I'm serious. What time does it start?"

"At nine."

"Well?"

"Well, what?"

"Get dressed, let's go! Unless you don't want to."

Connie ran down the hall to retrieve Jake's seldom-used Sunday shirt from the bottom of the when-you-get-to-it ironing basket. Ronnie bounced on his bare bottom, then scooted off the end of the bed and went streaking after her.

Maria's father chuckled as Ginny removed her hand. The spirit child folded her arms indignantly. She was not amused!

Mayville, 7:15 a.m.

Del's alarm was set for 8 a.m. but he'd been awake since seven, becoming more and more depressed. He hated Christmas! Well, not all of them, but certainly this one. He hadn't bothered putting up a tree or lights outside. Everything was different now. That's what he really hated ... change.

The first change had come with Sundays. It used to be that all businesses in town closed for the entire day, except for the coffee shop at the bus depot. It made Sunday special. Sure, he opened up at times for people with medical emergencies but that didn't happen too often. He and Virginia would sit in their favorite pew at church, and afterwards she would set the table with her best china and serve a fantastic dinner. It was "their" day.

Then, the area began growing like crazy. An Albertson's store came in which stayed open on Sundays and people certainly responded to the extra shopping day. The competition for the almighty dollar was incredible. More and more stores began opening up to cash in on the Sunday trade. Reluctantly, Del decided to open from noon to 5, to see what would happen. It proved to be one of his busiest days, and in general his business flourished. Before long Del was so busy that he'd end up racing home around three o'clock to wolf down those nice Sunday dinners. After a while, Virginia didn't bother putting out the china. Sunday was still "their" day. They just didn't spend much of it together.

But Virginia understood.

When Del's competitors also began staying open later he decided to extend store hours from 8 a.m. to 8 p.m., instead of the 10-to-6 schedule the store had been on for years. This meant hiring and supervising more help, and working longer hours in the pharmacy. Eventually, Del had to hire a part-time pharmacist so he could have an occasional day off. Yet he seldom went anywhere except to meetings at the Legion Hall. For the most part, he was worn out. He had more and more money, but less and less time or inclination to spend it.

"Wouldn't it be fun to go to England?" Virginia had asked one spring day after seeing a man win a trip on The Price is Right.

"We're so busy at the store. I couldn't possibly get away. Maybe next fall," he'd told her. Again, she understood.

That fall Virginia was all ecstatic about planning a trip to Hawaii for their anniversary in January. Then the shoe repair shop next to the drugstore closed down and Del had his heart set on expanding. He promised they'd go the following spring.

"Hawaii will still be there," she'd said. So understanding!

"I hear San Francisco is beautiful this time of year," Virginia had coaxed in March. "I've always wanted to ride the cable cars."

All Del could think of was completion of the planning and ordering for his newly expanded toy section. "Sure," he'd said. They'd go as soon as the remodeling was finished.

Virginia acknowledged that running a business was very demanding and tried not to show her disappointment.

The remodeling took longer than he had anticipated, but by late summer the new, improved toy section was looking great. All Del's hard work paid off. It was a tremendous success. Then one day, after the January clearance sales, Del noticed that Virginia seemed to have lost her spunk. A bad case of the "post-holiday blues," he thought. Still it wasn't like her, so he mentioned it to their doctor one day on the telephone.

"She needs to get away," the doctor said.

Del decided it was time. "How about you and me going on a little trip? To England maybe?"

"I don't think so," Virginia said, unenthusiastically. "We'd have to get blood tests and passports. Sounds like a lot of bother just for a couple of weeks."

"How about Hawaii? Can't you just see me in a grass skirt? Or there's those cable cars in San Francisco, maybe we could even try Disneyland? You know, 'California here we come.'"

"It doesn't sound as good as it used to," she admitted with a shrug. "Maybe next spring."

"Okay, I'll wait, watch and hope," he said, aiming one of her favorite phrases back at her, adding a wink and a hug.

By the end of March, Virginia had no energy.

"Probably a bit anemic," the doctor said. Still he ordered extensive blood tests.

The tests came back … Leukemia!

Del was crazy with worry. Virginia was surprisingly calm. After each radiation treatment Del eagerly asked, "What else can we try?"

In August, when the last of her hair fell out, Virginia said, "That's enough!"

"How long do we have?" he asked, frantically.

"I honestly don't know," the doctor said. "Let's look toward spring."

Virginia died December 29th.

The change coming in 1966 was called Valleyhills Mall. With its completion and the new freeway extension, trips into The City would be quicker and easier. People were already shopping away from their small-town stores. Originally this had meant they were coming more often to his. Yet realistically, Del knew that the novelty of the mall would pull people away from him by this time next year. He wasn't looking forward to that change at all.

Del's alarm went off. He deliberately knocked it off the nightstand. Virginia's picture fell too. The glass cracked. He nearly fell out of bed grabbing it off the floor. He ran a finger along the glass fracture hoping it would bleed, like his soul bled, and his heart. When it didn't, he propped the picture up against the box of Kleenex on the table and stared at it. Where was she now, this love of his life?

All he'd been taught about Heaven was of little comfort to him. He missed her, needed her, wanted her, and thinking of her floating around somewhere out of reach was more than he could bear. What was he supposed to do now?

His store ran like a well-oiled machine. Heck today, he didn't need to go in at all if he chose not to. He could go to church, but didn't feel like it. No one would notice my absence in either place, he thought. Covering his head with a pillow, Del rolled into a piteous lump. Sleep did not return.

His brain began spinning speculations. Del pondered what had happened at his store the evening before: the lost-hankie episode with the young woman, big-hearted Harvey with his kidding around, and the conversation in the truck about how Jean Martin had risen to the occasion, and was doing all she could to help Maria and her son. Besides seeing that they had food and shelter, she must have sent four hundred flyers to churches all over California and Arizona hoping that somehow Maria's husband would receive the message. It wasn't cheap, and Jean didn't exactly have buckets of bucks sitting around. She was just determined to help, and was good at it.

Next, Del's mind drifted to conversations he'd had with other customers. Carol Brown came to mind. She'd moved to Mayville as a kid. Heck, he'd known her since the chicken-pox days. She was usually witty and optimistic. That Saturday afternoon, though, Carol had been down in the dumps and horribly embarrassed, quietly taking him aside to ask if there was any way she could have a thirty-day store credit so she could purchase a few Christmas gifts.

Credit wasn't a problem; Del was just mystified when she requested that he not tell her husband. Finally he remembered. Carol's husband Randy was one of the "Forgotten Fifty," who'd been laid off from the mine last summer and were still unemployed because contract negotiations were deadlocked. Carol said he was terribly discouraged because it was Christmastime and he was broke. Something in the way she spoke about her husband, the sad, distant ring of her words troubled Del tremendously.

What a pity! Randy was a darn good mechanic. Too bad he couldn't find something to tide them over until the mine picked up again. "But there's nothing I can do about it," Del rationalized aloud.

"Call Harvey."

The words came clearly to his mind. He removed the pillow, thinking he needed more oxygen.

"Call Harvey."

The words came again. He sat halfway up in bed to listen again. Nothing happened, but since he was wide-awake, he got out of bed. "Might as well go to church. Nothing better to do," he grumbled.

The words came again while he was shaving.

"Call Harvey."

"Great! Now I'm insane!" he remarked to the mirror. He felt a strange mixture of amusement and anxiety and was mentally preparing a case for denial when he heard the words a fourth time.

"For crying out loud, why should I call Harvey?" he yelled at the ceiling. As soon as he asked, Del knew why. He rinsed off the razor, rubbed off the last of the shaving cream and wiped his face dry.

Ginny lowered her hand from the screen.

"Morning, Harvey! Did I wake you?" Del felt a bit guilty. "Sorry. Anyway, what I called about was this. I know someone who would be perfect for fitting that tractor of yours with snow equipment, like you said you wanted to do. He's a pretty fair mechanic, and he's got time right now. His name's Brown. Randy Brown. I wish I'd taken my car to him instead of to Moyd's! Hold on while I get you the number." He rapidly fumbled through the phone book. Half an hour later, he was on his way church.

The spirit child smiled. "Can I send a message too, Ginny?"

"We can ask permission. Can you tell me why you'd like to?"

A tender recollection caused the little spirit's countenance to glow. "When Suzannah was here we were best of best friends. We couldn't go to earth together but were so excited that we could be sisters. Then we heard sisters there don't always get along, so Suzannah made me a beautiful name and wrote it in her heart, to somehow bring back our forever feelings. It means: Heavenly angel that brings joyous news."

"Nice! And you're afraid Suzannah won't remember, or tell your folks in time?"

The spirit child nodded, concerned. "She's got lots of worries."

"All right. We'll ask for permission if things don't improve soon."

The viewing screen changed again. Ginny sat down comfortably. The spirit child crawled onto her lap and nodded her approval toward the scene.

Hometown, 8:30 a.m.

Suzannah slammed the car door so hard a large chunk of snow avalanched down the windshield. She couldn't believe it; didn't want to believe it. Try as she might, she could not find the shopping bag with her father's gift in it. It wasn't in the car. "Please let it be in my room," she implored out loud, yet she knew it couldn't be unless her mom had taken it inside. Suzannah had been dropped off at her neighbor Debbie's house right after shopping. She hadn't gone home first. Despair swelled in her stomach as she stumbled up the carport steps into the duplex.

"Don't forget to stomp off the snow," her mother called from the kitchen too late. A frosty trail had been tromped down the hallway and continued into Suzannah's room. She belly-flopped onto her bed, wailing into her pillow.

Carol Brown dropped the apple she was peeling to hurry down the short hall. "What's wrong, honey? Did you get hurt coming home?"

Suzannah shook her head but didn't remove it from the pillow, or cease the sobbing.

"Are you sick?"

Another headshake.

"Did you and Debbie have a fight?"

Nothing but tears came from her daughter. Sitting on the bed, Carol insisted, "Suzannah, please look at me and tell me what's wrong."

Suzannah opened her mouth; another wrenching wave of anguish escaped and she fell face first into her pillow again. Carol knew her 12-year-old would have to come up for air soon, and since a pillowcase can absorb only so much, her next move was to get a box of tissues. When she returned, she sat down again, resting her hand lovingly on Suzannah's back.

Twenty minutes and half a box later Suzannah sat up, blew her nose and tried to explain between gasps for breath. "When we shopped, I—I found a cool pres-ent for D-Dad?"

"Yes?" her mother said, coaxing.

"W-Well, it's gone! L-lost! I looked everywhere. It's gone!"

"Did you take it to Debbie's?"

"No," Suzannah whined. "L-last n-night I was telling her about what I g-got. Then I couldn't remember seeing the bag in the c-car when you dropped me off, or where I put it after the store. I was so w-worried; I didn't sleep all night. Then I got s-scared because her Dad snores real l-loud, and I ran home r-right after breakf-fast, which was half-cooked, eggy French t-toast. I almost b-barfed! When I got here I checked in the c-c-car and, and ..." the sobs began building again, "it's not there!" Suzannah put her face in her hands, another emotional earthquake hit.

Carol put her arm around the shuddering shoulders. Of all the years they needed Christmas to go smoothly this was the one, and it wasn't co-operating! "Honey, we can get him something else. What did you buy?"

"H-hankies."

"Hankies?"

"Yeah. Three n-nice big wh-white ones. I b-bought 'em

with my own m-money! It was supposed to b-be a surprise." Again the hands covered the face.

Suddenly she looked up, a little calmer. "H-hey, if we go back to Mayville and look around the p-parking lot maybe we'll find 'em." She looked for a hopeful sign of agreement from her mother.

"Suz, you saw how much it snowed last night, worst storm of the year and more due tonight! The snowplows have barely started clearing the main roads. There's lots of drifting. I don't know if we'll be able to drive three miles to church, let alone driving fifteen into Mayville to look for a sack of hankies."

Suzannah sobbed miserably. She knew her mom was right, but darn it anyway, now her secret was ruined, her plan was ruined and Christmas would be ruined.

"We'll get him something. We've got almost a week."

Shaking, Suzannah curled up on the end of the bed with her pillow. Carol pulled the heavy patchwork quilt down to cover her.

"No more Saturday-night sleep-overs," she said to herself, as she sopped puddles off the carpet, leftovers from Suzannah's previously snowy path.

"Poor Suzannah! She lost her hankies and she cried. Maria found the hankies and she cried. Hankies cause a lot of trouble!"

"Don't blame the hankies for the tears, little one. Sometimes bad moments create new opportunities for blessings."

Mayville, 9:00 a.m.

Maria was relieved when Jean left for church. All morning she had tried to appear cheerful, hopeful. With Jean gone, Maria sank into the padded rocking chair, overwhelmed by unbidden memories of the past year that came like ghosts, haunting her, rekindling her grief. Little Carlos played nearby. How much he had grown since her mother had last seen him. What a terrible year it had been!

She had grown up in the heat of Mexico. It never snowed there. It was a place of dirt, sweat and hard work. She had seen her father move up from the position of field hand to foreman for one of the three farms owned by Lajeda & Co. He had earned this honor through years of working with crops as though they were his own. Maria worked beside him whenever Mama freed her from household chores or from tending a younger sister, Elena. She kept pace with her older brother, Alejandro, when it came to planting or weeding the long rows and her father good-naturedly teased the boy.

Alejandro never thought it was funny and often sulked when she was near. Maria pretended not to notice. She wanted her father's approval, not Alejandro's. This made him angrier. If she had taken this jealousy seriously would she still be home?

Home. Maria sat tearfully rocking as she recalled moving from the one-room dwelling of the worker's quarters to the two-bedroom cottage by the huge storage shed. It was a real house, and to her seven-year-old eyes seemed like a mansion with a kitchen, living room and a bathroom of its own. Many important events had occurred there. Birthdays. Christmases. Holy Communion parties.

For hers, Mama custom-made a beautiful, white cotton dress and veil with lace and delicate embroidery. The intricate work brought Mama great satisfaction. For Quinceañera, her coming-of-age party at fifteen, they had worked together to create an elaborate dress that perfectly fit Maria's maturing figure. "Where has my little girl gone?" Papa had asked, spinning her around like a lady at a grand ball.

Eduardo Sanchez was introduced to her in that house, at Alejandro's wedding. He was shorter, of slighter build than her brother, but had a kind heart, pleasant manners and a very romantic way with words. He would sweetly say into her ear, "Todas las estrellas brillan en tus ojos y me llevan al cielo." All the stars shine in your eyes and lead me to heaven.

Their own wedding was celebrated in that home, with

colored lights and hours of dancing. Maria wore a wedding gown of her own design, adding lace and exquisite handwork that had taken her weeks to complete. Even greater joy filled the house a year later when Carlos was born there. Mama had been the midwife, and Maria remembered how her parents held her tiny son swaying together in a dance of devotion.

Within two years, though, unimaginable sadness found its way to that house. In March, Papa died suddenly, while resting on the porch step.

Then came the fight ...

Alejandro, who'd become foreman after their father's death, was not liked because of his temper. Production was down. He needed someone to blame. He chose Eduardo, and because Eduardo was married to Maria, the old animosity arose like a monster from a black grave. It struck with deadly accuracy one afternoon in April.

Alejandro had returned from purchasing seed for the farm. He'd bartered well and had nearly two hundred dollars left. He intended to give it to the general manager as a display of competence. On the way from his small office in the storage shed, Alejandro bragged to Maria and Eduardo who were standing outside. Then he went into the house.

Somewhere along the way, Alejandro put down the zippered bag that held the money. When he returned to his office, it couldn't be found. He ran back into the house to search, cursing with each breath.

"It's good that Mama's not home," Maria whispered. Their father had never allowed anyone to speak words of that kind around his wife.

When Alejandro didn't find the bag in the house, he ran again to the shed and began throwing things. Wild-eyed he appeared in the doorway, pointed to Eduardo, shaking with anger. "You stole the money!"

"What?"

"There is no other explanation. Until I left from talking to you, I had it. Now it's gone. You have stolen it and you will be punished!"

"You're crazy!" Maria had protested. "He would not do that."

Alejandro raised his hand as if he would strike her. "If he hasn't stolen the money, then you have."

Eduardo rose up between them. Alejandro shook his head in disgust. "A real man doesn't have his woman steal!"

Eduardo rebuked him. "We have not stolen your money. You must have spent more than you thought!"

Alejandro grabbed his brother-in-law by the shirt and jerked him forward, "You are a thief and you will leave now! Today! Or I will call the police!"

Maria pulled down on her brother's strong arm, "Stop this! We did not take the money. You can't make us leave! Mama needs us!"

Alejandro loosened his grip on Eduardo, and turned on Maria. "I am the boss here now. I say who stays, and I don't want thieves around! You stole our father's love from me. Now you do this to disgrace me. You will leave or be arrested!"

"The police won't believe you!"

Alejandro took a different approach. "The police don't have to. The Lajedas will hear of the scandal and throw us all out. Mama will die of a broken heart and it will be your fault!"

"You viper! You can't chase Maria from the family," Eduardo snarled in her defense.

Alejandro roared, "To this family there is no Maria!"

Even now at Jean's, the memories tightened Maria's throat to the point that every sob choked her. She tried to push the ugliness out of her mind. It would not leave.

The night they left the farm, Mama was told it was for an opportunity in the United States. She wept into little Carlos' blanket, and begged Maria to stay.

"They have to go, Mama," Alejandro said, pulling her away from Maria's embrace.

Maria had looked up at him, eyes pleading for reconsideration. He tightened his hold around their Mama.

The little family traveled with a group of migrant workers in an old school bus from farm to farm from then until June. Children fought. Babies wailed. Mothers argued. Sometimes the bus broke down and they were late getting to a picking site. By then most of the cabins were taken and they were once again crowded, cramped and miserable. Maria thought she would lose her mind. She had never been so dirty and hungry!

As Carlos played that morning at Jean's, it was hard to imagine he was the same baby who got sick last July, becoming limp in her arms; his lips turning purple. She'd screamed for help, begging God not to take her child.

The memories beyond that continued, painfully vivid. The ambulance. The hospital. She did not understand what the doctor said. A young missionary interpreted, explaining that surgery had to be done immediately.

Carlos had to stay in the hospital for many weeks. Before he was released Eduardo had to leave to look for winter employment in California or Arizona. How else would they survive? She sobbed like a frightened child, weeks of hospital exhaustion taking their toll. He would come back for her soon. He held her, whispering again of those heavenly stars, and loved her, and promised!

Now it was Christmas, and there was no home, no husband, and no celebration in her heart. What could she do? She had nothing to give to Jean or her son.

Her father's words came into her mind, crowding in on her sorrow.

'No es tiempo para llorar, es tiempo para trabajar da gracias por el trabajo, y hazlo!' It is not time for tears. It is time for work. Give thanks for work, and then do it!

How those get-busy phrases had annoyed her as a youth! Papa's face looked stern when he said it, but his happy eyes betrayed him. Still, she knew that he meant what he said. The words came a second time.

A wave of comfort helped her think clearly; to search for a solution. The hankies ... that's it!

Maria's father lowered his hand from the screen.
"You're a good daddy," the spirit child said.
"Thank you," he smiled, patted her hand and walked away.

The spirit child turned to Ginny. "Why did it help Maria to hear that?"

"It helped her not to give up. It reminded her that she is not powerless, that she can do something small while she waits for something big to happen."

"Waiting feels like a long time on earth, doesn't it?"

"Yes, quite often. Down there they forget that mortality is merely a drop of eternity."

"I think waiting will be one of my Life Challenges."

"I wouldn't be surprised," Ginny said, with a grin.

San Vega, 9:20 a.m.

Connie couldn't help smiling. It was hard to tell who had the worst case of church wiggles, the three-year old with a baggie full of Cheerios, or the thirty year-old tugging uncomfortably on his necktie. It didn't matter. They were all at church together for the first time since Ronnie had been blessed as a baby. She was thrilled!

Jake fidgeted, trying to pay attention. He sensed it was important. But that blasted tie was driving him nuts! The Christmas program was not spectacular, but nice. Jake got a big kick out of the little kids who sang "Away in a Manger," most of all the little girl who picked her nose all the way through it. Connie poked him in the ribs hard for snickering. But hey, it wasn't his kid, so why not laugh? He was actually enjoying the meeting. Still he had no clue about the reason that he'd felt so compelled to attend.

Ronnie turned around on the bench and was playing "grab fingers" with a little girl about his age in a red velvet dress, who sat on the bench behind them. When she suddenly caught his hand, he let out a giggle-snort combination.

"Shhh," Connie said as she turned him around, whispered firmly into his ear and made him fold his arms. It lasted about a minute, and then he was back at it again.

He's my kid all right, Jake grinned. Sitting reverently through church was not a Boyer strong point, never had been. Again Connie turned Ronnie around.

A pretty lady with red hair was getting ready to sing *O Holy Night*. The introduction was played, she took a deep breath, opened her mouth and ...

"AaaaEeeeeOWWW!" screamed Ronnie.

The people sitting closest to the Boyers jumped about four inches. The pianist crashed a few keys. The singer stood dumbfounded, her mouth agape. Everyone looked around in surprise. Everyone, except the little red velvet Delilah on the bench behind Ronnie who was holding a handful of his hair.

The mothers exchanged horror-filled glances. Ronnie continued his fire engine wail. The little girl received a slap on the hand, and she started wailing too. Connie felt ready to cry herself. Jake scooped up his son, winked at his wife, and headed out of the chapel to the foyer where he could at least talk to his son above a whisper and hopefully calm him down. He heard the music start up again and saw that the little girl's mother had made the same hasty retreat. She immediately took up residence on a moss-colored couch that was placed, probably for just such emergencies next to a burnt-orange overstuffed chair and an end table with a fake fern. Once there, Delilah's mommy began pulling stuff out of a colorful cotton tote bag. Apologetically she offered Ronnie one of the graham crackers she had brought to bribe her kid into being reverent. Peace was achieved immediately.

"Imagine how fast wars would end if everyone sat down right away and shared some graham crackers," Jake said, in a low voice.

"At my house, it works every time."

Soon both kids were looking at a flannel storybook, so Jake wandered about twenty feet away to look at the bulletin board down the hallway. There was a list of missionary addresses, a poster about the New Year's Eve Dance, and ... Jake froze. There in front of him was a picture of that *guy*, the one from yesterday, sitting next to a small boy in a hospital bed. It was on a flyer that read:

"Please Help Me Find My Daddy."

Goose bumps rolled down Jake's spine as he read the details of the family's dilemma. He knew where to find this guy! At least, he knew where to start looking.

———

"Look at the beautiful lady! Who is she?"
"I believe it's Patricia, all dressed up for church."
"I wish I could tell her how pretty she looks!"
"Don't worry. She probably knows."

———

The City, 10:00 a.m.

Heads turned as Patricia Watterson, the picture of perfection in a dress of baby-blue velvet, gracefully glided down the aisle to her favorite pew and sat as delicately as a butterfly alighting on a flower. Her children, Tiffany and Thomas, followed closely behind, stopping at the edge of the bench while she was seated, then ever so gently coming to sit by her side. It was this way every Sunday, as though they had practiced it at home. A bit later her husband rather unceremoniously plunked down beside them.

It was hard not to notice they were being noticed, and normally Patricia would have reveled in the attention. However, today she was extremely tired and hoped her eyes didn't look puffy. She felt pensive about her part in the Christmas presentation, wondering if her masterpiece would be appreciated.

For weeks she had been preparing to recite "I Heard the Bells on Christmas Day" which no doubt would have been the highlight of the program. Her plans had changed. Instead she would read a creation of her own, born of a restless, wearisome night, following the most harrowing Saturday of her life. She had tried to forget about the people she had seen at the Hope For Life Center; tried to drown the day's memory with mugs of hot chocolate. Still it had persisted.

Expecting to find winos and haggard old ladies, she had not been disappointed, there had been a few of those huddled on cots here and there. What Patricia had not expected to see were families, especially not families with little children. There had been plenty of those, too. It was unbelievable.

"I have two presents for children," she told the director of the Center, an old school chum of Robert's, handing over the packages that Harvey had given to her outside the drugstore.

"I appreciate that," he said, sincerely, "but it'll be hard to choose which two of the seventeen to give them to."

"Seventeen?"

"Yup, and that number could easily double by Christmas Eve. We usually get a few new things donated for our toy box, and tell the kids to share. Feeding them is our biggest priority. I sure appreciate what you've done tonight. Forty-six bucks? That's great! Every dollar means a dinner, ya know."

"So I've heard," she said, weakly, realizing that Robert must have put in extra.

Later, with her family asleep, Patricia sat in the lavishly decorated living room feeling troubled. She rationalized, "There's no more I can do for those people." Yet sleep evaded her. She'd finished her fifth mug of hot chocolate, and felt drowsy enough to go up to bed, when she was halted by a sudden urge to write a poem.

She hadn't written much since high school, though she did regularly peruse the rhyming Hallmark sentiments with each new season. Superb spontaneity poured from her pen with amazing ease. Feelings flowed freely and fervently, and when finished, she knew the poem must be shared. Robert would be so surprised! Of course she would have to *read* it. Certainly no one would expect it to be memorized when it was so newly created! Feeling like a new mother bringing her newborn to church for the first time; she anxiously awaited her turn.

The woman in front of her turned around and smiled. Patricia smiled back. The man in the next pew also nodded and smiled. Again, she smiled and nodded back. She glanced behind without completely turning, startled to see others looking at her with an air of expectation. Panic gripped her heart. Demurely she reached back with her hand, as though rubbing her neck and felt to make certain. Zipper was fine. Thank goodness! Still her children stared at her as though in disbelief too. What could it be?

Finally, Robert leaned over and whispered, "Honey, you're up!"

Lost in thought, she had missed her cue. She stood abruptly, dumping a hymnbook from her lap onto the floor with a loud thud. How humiliating! She carefully maneuvered around it, and walked with poise to the pulpit, taking a deep breath as inconspicuously as possible.

Patricia recited,

> In the little town of Marleyville the bells had
> been silent for years.
> The people were all too busy to care, stifled
> with suspicion and fears.
> Then one Christmas Eve, a woman forlorn,
> wearing a tattered coat,
> Came to find shelter and food if she could.
> Though her chances were quite remote.
> She asked an old innkeeper for room and rest.
> But he angrily said, "Not tonight!"
> The storekeeper said, "You scare buyers away.
> You must leave. You're a terrible sight."
> She told passersby she was hungry.
> They said, "We've no money to spare."
> Then she thought, they need love to ring in their
> hearts,
> Then they'd probably care.
> If I got the bells in the steeple to chime,
> I'm sure it would touch every heart,
> And maybe they'd see it's a blessing to give.
> At least it would be a start!
> So the traveler forlorn found the tiny church and
> opened the dusty door.
> She prayed, "I'm so tired, but Lord give me
> strength. I need a little more."
> Then she climbed up the stairs to the steeple
> And pulled on the gnarled old rope.
> And the bells did ring out with a cling-clang-
> ing shout
> Which filled the poor woman with hope.
> The music swelled through the hills and dells

And touched everyone where they lived.
And they joyfully ran to the church on the hill
To see what they needed to give.
The innkeeper said, "Come eat and rest.
I *do* have a room, it is one of my best!"
Then with the dawn she was suddenly gone, or
so the story tells …
But on top of the pillow where she had lain
down her head,
They found two tiny silver bells!
Ring out! Ring out! It's Christmastide; listen to the
story of the bells.
And take care of strangers who come into your
midst,
For they just might be angells!

Patricia looked up, triumphant. She had never seen so many wide-eyed looks in her life. They *did* appreciate it! Including Robert, who was looking down, one hand covering his face. He was shaking; obviously deeply touched.

"What will she think of next?" Patricia heard one obviously immature teenager ask another as she walked back to her pew.

"Just wait and see!" she whispered. Inspiration number two had descended upon her mind with clarity and brilliance.

Mayville, 11:00 a.m.

Del was out of breath when he caught up to Jean after church. She had half a block's start on him.

"Jean!" he called, hoping to slow her down. It worked.

"I wanted to tell you that your song was nice."

Jean half-giggled, shaking her head. "It would have been better if Mabel Crane had showed up," she said, a note of exasperation in her voice. "It was supposed to be a duet. I've never been a soloist!"

"You were today, and it turned out fine."

"If you say so. But if people have nightmares tonight, they'll have me to blame. I shudder to think about it!" She shook her head again. "So, how've you been? I'm surprised to see you walking."

"All right, mostly. My car's in the shop. Was supposed to be finished last night."

"You left it at Moyd's?"

"How'd you guess?"

"A nasty rumor. Makes me glad I don't drive."

They walked on in silence until Del spoke up. "Mind if I ask a personal question?"

"Ooh, I hate those," Jean said, smiling. "It usually means someone's about to get nosy in a nice way, or ask my opinion on something controversial. Which is it?"

"The nosy-but-nice kind. I know you've been trying to find Maria's husband, but isn't there other family, like parents?"

"Yes. Maria's mother is living with Maria's older brother. Her father died last spring. Why?"

"Nothing. It's just that I know you're doing a lot for her and all, but she seemed awfully sad when she was in the store last night. If she was my daughter, I'd want to know where she was."

Jean's smile faded into a solemn look. "You can't always keep track of kids nowadays, Del."

What a fool I am, he thought, remembering that Jean's daughter Betsy took off five years ago, and there'd been no word from her since.

"I'm sorry. I didn't mean ... I mean, what I meant was ..."

"It's okay, Del. I know what you meant. It's my fault. What I should have said was, yes, Maria has tried to contact her mother. There's a problem though, some trouble with her brother. She's written but we don't know whether her mother has received the letters and not answered, or whether she's even received them in the first place."

"That's terrible!"

"Yes. But right now, the one she needs to hear from most is her husband."

Del began to wonder if Jean was setting herself up for more grief by getting so attached to Maria and her son. "What if her husband doesn't show up?"

"We'll do what we are doing now, living each day as it comes."

Del walked the next block trying to get up courage, then carefully said, "Jean, you get too involved sometimes. I worry. This whole situation looks like a guaranteed heart-breaker to me."

Taken aback, Jean was ready to tell him that he had a lot of gall to say such a thing, but stopped. The look in his eyes told her that he meant it out of concern for her. It took her a while to think of an answer, then she said, reflectively, "One thing that being around Virginia taught me, was that a sad heart is better than an empty one. Yes, it will hurt like the dickens when Maria goes. But it feels so good to be needed again, and when little Carlos gives me a hug, it's wonderful! So I intend to enjoy every minute of it."

He shook his head. "You're amazing, Jean. I'm sure Maria appreciates it. I owe you a lot too."

She patted him on the shoulder, smiling, "I'll send you a bill on the 39th!"

Hometown, 12:30 p.m.

Carol Brown looked in on her sleeping daughter. Moments later she returned with a warm washcloth and draped it gently over Suzannah's swollen eyes. "You'd better get up honey, or you won't be able to sleep tonight," she said, smoothing the tousled bangs on her child's sweaty forehead.

Suzannah moaned, rolled ever so slowly onto her side and struggled to lift her eyelids. Each felt like a swollen balloon covered with hot sand. Even gently rubbing her long dark lashes against a wet cloth to loosen the salty grit was painful, but necessary if she hoped to see her way to the bathroom. Little by little she succeeded until she could clearly see the smiles that greeted her from across the room.

There her little family of favorite dolls sat patiently on the top two rows of the dark pine bookcase she had inherited from Great-Granny Brown. Each one was cherished. In many ways they had become substitute siblings. And plain-named Suzannah Brown, who was nicknamed Suz (never Suzy) or occasionally ZannahSu, if her dad was feeling nutty, had rechristened her treasured playthings with more glamorous titles than their store-bought labels.

To her, Raggedy Ann was Annabella Anastasia

Ragglesworth, and Raggedy Andy was named Andrew
Taylor Ragglesworth. The doll that blew kisses and the one
who clapped went from Kissy and Patti-Cake to Kristella
Kaylee Smooch and Pattina Cathleena Cuddles. The home-
made work-sock monkey with the mischievous grin became Mr. Morris Monkeyshines and the braided yarn doll
was dubbed Cinderella because, hey, even a plain girl with
stringy hair deserves to hope!

Last year's Tammy doll was Tamileah Trueheart, and
Suzannah claimed not to mind that most other girls received
Barbie dolls instead. This was a big relief to her mother, who
felt that Barbie dolls had a snobby, conceited look about
them and a figure a dirty old man must have dreamt up!

Suzannah's Ruthie doll with molded plastic hair was Ruth
Naomi Esther, and her dad had suggested the bride doll be
called Marie Antoinette because she had obviously lost her
head over some guy. Suzannah had humored him a bit by
using Antoinette as the bride's middle name, but actually
called her Victoria. And of course, she couldn't call her
sweet baby doll with go-to-sleep eyes, Drink 'n Wet.
Precious Darling Love-alot sounded better, but Suz simply
called her Lovey.

Exactly why she was so fond of names with a flair,
Suzannah didn't know. The reason eluded her. Somehow it
seemed important. She dearly loved these fantasy friends
she'd been given over the years, yet felt one was missing.
Another face was supposed to claim the last extraordinary
name that was engraved in her mind. It was so treasured
that she shared it with no one, hadn't even written it in her
diary, and had never found a doll in any store that it was
meant to grace. Too late now. Suzannah sighed. She was
supposed to be beyond the dolly stage. She was almost a
teenager! A bit reluctantly she diverted her attention to the
posters on the wall around the dresser in the corner opposite the bookcase.

A strip of white butcher paper 5 feet in length was tacked
to the wall above the dresser that sat at an angle across the
far corner of the room. The paper was used so the old
plaster walls wouldn't chip from tacks or tape. From it
peered the faces of her future. David Cassidy, Bobby

Sherman, and Bobby Vinton were part of a magazine-clipped photo collection sent by her cousin Mary Beth Alice, who was going off to college where the "real men" were and couldn't be bothered with "such nonsense" anymore.

There were ladies too: Grace Kelly, Julie Andrews, Patty Duke and that Gidget girl, to name a few along with musical groups like the Supremes, the Beach Boys, Herman's Hermits, the Monkees, and even one of those Beatle-guys who had recently been on the Ed Sullivan Show. She thought they were cute, but her dad thought they were too radical to amount to much.

He was always giving wacky opinions. When he saw Barbra whats-her-name's T.V. special he said, "She's good enough to sing warts off a frog!"

"Dad, frogs don't have any warts!" Suz had protested.

"Did a good job, didn't she!"

Where had this funny Dad gone, she wondered, looking at a family picture on her dresser. Lately his smile was hidden behind a cloud. She missed it. These days Dad was real ornery, not having enough to do. The lay-off was supposed to last a month, and for that long he'd stayed busy. Heck, it was like a vacation to him, he'd said, even though his paycheck was smaller. When there was no steady work after a month was over, he became worried. By the end of the third month, when all his odd jobs were finished and he had to file for unemployment, the grumbling began.

Mom still had her part-time job at the bank and made arrangements to work full time. Dad didn't like this at all and Suzannah often overheard them disagreeing about why she did that when he was going to get his job back any day. He went to union meetings and came home frustrated, shouting about idiotic dispute proposals. Mom would tell him to please lower his voice. He'd say she didn't understand and storm out, slamming the door. As time went on, the Dad part of him seemed lost in the worry part of him. When Suz spoke to him, he'd look right at her, but his dark green eyes were focused beyond her somewhere. He watched television more than ever and the arguing increased.

She forced herself to look away from the family photo. She couldn't think about it right now. She'd cried enough for one day. Suzannah's gaze fell back to the dolls. Some parts of childhood she would miss, but she would never give her babies away, and remained convinced that somewhere in MaryBeth Alice's house there was a box with dolls in it!

"Come help me make the cookies," Mom called from the kitchen, interrupting her reverie.

Mom making cookies on Sunday morning? This she had to see. She slid off her bed and hurried to wash her face. The warm water marvelously soothed away the last traces of the morning's tearful deluge. But as she looked into the mirror the memory of the lost hankies threatened to start the flood again. What was she going to do? With all her might, she pushed that question out of her mind. "What happened to church today?" she asked, rounding the corner from the hallway.

"You were so exhausted and upset, I didn't think you were up to a three-mile walk in knee-deep snow."

Suzannah ran to the kitchen window and looked out at the driveway. A huge wind-whipped snowdrift held their car hostage in the carport. Her footprints from that morning had long been filled in. A newer set of footprints went through the fresh white powder. "Where's Dad?"

"Went to Church," Carol called out over the whining of the hand mixer.

"He walked? Why didn't you stop him?"

The mixer came to a halt. "Suzannah, have you ever known anyone who could stop your dad if he wanted to do something bad enough?"

"No. But maybe we should have gone with him."

Carol shook her head slightly, and turned away, starting the mixer up again.

Now Suzannah knew they'd had another argument. She felt angry. "Dang that union anyway! It's ruined everything. I wish Dad would tell the mine owners and the bosses to take a flying leap and get a job somewhere where there aren't any lay-offs!" Suzannah hit her fist on the table, causing two cookies to fall off the cooling rack.

"Take a flying leap?" Mother asked, with an odd smile. "Where did you learn that one?"

"At school."

"I can't believe the things kids come up with these days."

"That's the mild version. There's a wild version, but it's…"

"Not very ladylike. Yes, I've heard it. I wouldn't repeat it, if I were you."

"I know, it just makes me so mad about Dad. He said the other day that the main guy who has to end the layoff took his wife on a cruise for Christmas."

"That's only a rumor," her mother said, changing the subject. She'd already discussed the validity of it with her alarmingly angry husband earlier. There was no consoling him no matter what she said or did. She, too, was sick at heart just thinking about how bogged down the negotiations had become. The delays had turned her normally easy-going sweetheart into an anxious, easily irritated stranger. She was glad he had gone to church. She needed a break. "Hey kiddo, will you look in the top of the hall closet and see if there is any red ribbon left from your birthday? I thought it would be fun to tie a pretty bow around the little foil plates when we give the cookies away."

Suzannah dragged the kitchen stool down the hall and climbed up to look. The ribbon was buried under two layers of other stuff. It came tumbling down on top of her when she jerked the large spool of ribbon loose. She wasn't exactly hurt, though she did get konked on the head by a large cardboard tube with metal ends. "Mom?" she called out, "Can I throw the empty wrapping thing away?"

"What empty wrapping thing?"

"This one with metal ends. There's no paper on it, and it hit me on the head!"

Wiping her hands on a towel, Carol Brown came into the hall. She recognized the brown cylinder right away. "No, honey," she said, taking it tenderly away from her daughter. "We can't throw it away. It's Daddy's dream. Probably the biggest reason that he's so depressed."

"Why? Was he gonna make something out of it?"

"No, silly. Come to the table. I'll show you." Carol chuckled, prying one of the metal ends off the brown cylinder and pulling out several large, tightly rolled papers with blue lines and printing. She smoothed them into a neat pile on the coffee table in the small living room. "This is Daddy's dream house."

"A house? Oh, let me see, let me see."

Pointing to different locations as she talked, Carol explained, "This is the living room. See, it has a small bay window. And this is the kitchen. It has a snack bar!"

"With tall chairs?"

"Yup, four of them."

"Wow! Debbie's aunt has those. They're so cool!"

"And there's the bathroom. An extra door opens into our room."

Pointing across the page, Suzannah asked, "Is this my room?"

"Uh huh! And this little room can be a nurs … I mean, a sewing room. And the stairs here in the living room go down to a full basement."

"Not a crawl space?"

"Nope. Full basement! And we planned on putting a laundry room and family room down there."

"This is so neat. Why didn't you tell me?"

"Dad and I decided to keep quiet about it until we knew for sure that we could start building. A lot of the things we wanted when we got married haven't worked out. We thought this would give us a fresh start. Now with the lay-off it's out of the question. And since I don't make that much at the bank, we can't always pay all our bills on time, which hurts our credit rating, which is a thing that helps banks decide whether or not to give us a building loan. And if we don't have a loan, we can't build a house." She paused for a moment. "He wanted it so bad." Carol gently rolled up the papers and replaced the metal end on the cylinder. "I'll put this in my room so nobody else gets konked by it." She ruffled Suzannah's hair, then went to her room.

Suzannah sat in silence. She heard the sliding sound of her mom's closet door, saw her mom dabbing her eyes with the bottom corner of her apron as she returned to the kitchen. Now she wished more than ever that the layoff boss *would* take a flying leap and not to the Caribbean, but clear off the planet!

Mayville, 6:28 p.m.

Jean Martin had just finished washing the dinner dishes as the telephone rang. The voice on the other end said, "This is the operator. I have a collect call from Mr. Jake Boyer. Will you accept the charge?"

Monday, December 20, 1965

Hometown, 6:45 a.m.

Suzannah woke up Monday morning hoping that the snowplow had been up the road so the school bus could make it. Normally she'd wish like crazy that the bus couldn't make it. Not today. There were only three school days left before Christmas break, three fun days.

The whole school would be practicing the Christmas program they were going to perform Wednesday night. They'd been working on their songs in class for weeks, but now that all the students were singing together it sounded like a real choir. They were also going to wear their dad's or big brother's white shirts with black crepe paper bow ties and actually try to look like a real choir too.

In addition to that, Suzannah was going to be Mary in the nativity scene; a singular honor that nearly every 6th-grade girl desired. This year Suzannah had been selected. Maybe it was because of her long dark hair. Maybe it was because the teacher liked her, or maybe because she had the highest score on the last spelling test. She didn't know why or care why. She was just happy to be chosen.

She was to sit on the stage holding a blanket-wrapped doll while the rest of the school sang, "Silent Night." It was going to be an incredible sight with the spotlight shining directly on her, and the dark green curtains "flowing down behind her" as Mrs. Wray put it. Mrs. Wray, who had been her 3rd-grade teacher, was the teacher-director for the whole thing. She felt strongly that Suzannah's scene would be a "memorable moment leading to a picture-perfect finale," so it was bound to be neat.

Other than the program practice, they weren't doing much, just studying for the last spelling test, and finishing up artistic gifts for their families. Suzannah had already finished the Festive Drawer Freshener (a clove-covered apple), and the Shimmering Tree Trimming (a glitter-covered pine cone), and knew the spelling words, so she was hoping Miss Hawkins would let her work on a very special project.

She had this great idea to make a picture and poem about Dad's dream house, to let him know not to give up; that dreams *can* come true. She knew exactly how she wanted to draw it, and felt that if she explained how important it was, her teacher might allow her to go ahead with it, using some of the good art paper. Of course, it wouldn't be as good a present as hankies would have been, but she hoped it might cheer her Dad up a bit, and it would never have to be washed or ironed.

On Wednesday afternoon they planned to have a class party, a real pig-out where everyone could eat cookies, brownies, and chip 'n dip to their hearts delight. Then they'd play games and break open the papier-mâché elf piñata they'd made the week before. A few girls suggested having a 6th-grade dance. Suzannah had voted *against* it. She was sure to get stuck dancing with Jordan or Gordon Nordan and they drove her crazy!

Jordan was 13, a year older than his classmates. He'd had to repeat 6th grade because he'd been run over by a tractor the year before, got a fractured leg and missed a lot of school. Gordon was 11 and had been promoted from 4th to 6th grade because he was so smart, but he was also a smart aleck, and, if the rumors were true, the one who'd been driving the tractor. Sometimes these brothers were partners in crime. Other times, they made Cain and Abel look like the Bobbsey Twins. And though she'd never actually seen any, if there were ever boys with cooties, it was sure to be them!

One of their delights was tormenting girls, hiding their books, biting the eraser off their pencils, or flinging spit wads into their hair. Long hair can hold a lot of spit wads. Suzannah knew this all too well, though she had to admit that Jordan hadn't been his usual pranky self around her since the Hometown Holiday Parade.

This annual event was held the day after Thanksgiving and lasted half an hour if the participants walked slowly. It covered a four-block stretch from the elementary school to the front of Town Hall, where the Christmas lights on the town's fifty-year-old evergreen would be lit up, kids would be lined up to meet Santa, and parents would be filled up with coffee or cocoa provided by the American Legion.

The parade began with a good old horn-honking, siren-blaring salute from the local volunteer fire department as they showed off their new fire truck. This encouraged stragglers to get to the sides of the street so they wouldn't be run over. After that the high school drill team pranced down the street in little Santa's helper outfits. They stopped twice along the route to perform part of their latest routine to "Holly Jolly Christmas," then pranced onward. The last two, either the largest or the tallest girls carried a "Happy Holidays" banner. A new car from Hometown Motors followed with the mayor and his family who threw saltwater taffy to the crowd.

Afterward the elementary Tonette flute band played "Jingle Bells" over and over. The junior high band added "We Wish You a Merry Christmas" and "Deck the Halls," and then the high school marching band blasted a jazzy rendition of "Good King Wenceslas" and "Here Comes Santa Claus." Another new car from Hometown Motors carried a "ho-ho-ho-ing Santa Claus with a pretty Miss Hometown sitting beside him blowing kisses and throwing kisses (the chocolate kind). And it was over.

Everyone usually turned out for the parade no matter the weather and many people braved the crowds at Town hall. So in a gathering of this size it would be easy for a child to get separated from family members, especially a myopic 6-year-old with a particularly bad sense of direction: Nelldan Nordan.

Because their father was helping at the Hall, he had told the boys, Jordan, Gordon and Sheldon, age 8, to take care of their sister and make sure that she got to see Santa Claus. Jordan told Gordon to bring her along. Gordon told Sheldon to hang onto her even if he had to hold her hand. But Sheldon was eight. He wouldn't hold his sister's hand in public if his life depended on it. Besides, she disappeared so fast after the parade ended that he just assumed Jordan had taken her.

However, Nellie Nordan was not with Jordan, nor was she headed to Town Hall. Engrossed in the high-spirited chatter of the high school drill team and marching band, she turned around and followed as they traipsed back to the elementary school to board buses to go participate in the afternoon Christmas parade in The City.

As luck would have it, Suzannah and her mother, who had a bad headache, had decided to avoid the siege for Santa and settle for hot chocolate at home. They saw Nellie wandering around the school parking lot, lost and in tears.

"Poor little mother-less waif!" Carol Brown said, sympathetically.

"Mom, she knows me. I'll go catch her and take her back to the Hall, okay?"

"Good idea, Suz. Call me later if you need a ride home," she said, unlocking her car.

As she headed back to the festivities with Nellie Nordan, her new best friend, a frantic, very grateful, Jordan Nordan, met them. From then on his attitude toward Suzannah changed.

Now instead of teasing her with his brother, Suzannah caught him stealing shy glances at her in class and at church. Sometimes it gave her a cold shivery feeling. Sometimes it gave her a warm shivery feeling. Either way, the feelings were so mixed and those Nordan boys too unpredictable. If there was the slightest chance she'd have to dance with one of them at a class get-together, forget it!

Hometown, 6:55 a.m.

"Where's Dad?" Suzannah asked at breakfast, pulling on her knee socks.

"He got a call late last night about a job," her mom said. "He's going to be fixing someone's tractor this whole week. Isn't that great?"

"Dad has work? Outta sight! Now that's what he really needs for Christmas!"

Tuesday, December 21, 1965

Mayville, 6:30 a.m.

Del Jones nearly knocked everything off the nightstand again as he grabbed for the phone. "Hello," he croaked into the receiver.

"Good grief Del, thought you'd be up and at 'em by now."

"Harvey? What the … hey, it's 6:30 in the morning! Of course I'm not up yet. The sun isn't even up yet! Just you and the roosters. What's the matter?"

"Nothing's the matter. I wanted to thank you for sending Randy Brown my way. He's definitely the mechanic I've been lookin' for."

"That's great. See ya later, Harve."

"Now hang on a minute. There's more to tell. You'll never guess who called last night and asked me to play Santa for a shindig she's throwing."

"I give. Who?"

"My daughter-in-law, Patricia. Seems she's plannin' to gather some gifts and food for a homeless shelter and asked if we could donate toys, and if I wanted to wear my Santa suit and hand 'em out."

"It was a wrong number, Harve. There are lots of Patricias out there, ya know."

"No, I'm tellin' ya Del, it was *our* Patricia. She didn't actually talk to *me*, but Enid is good at voices and she was certain."

"Well I'll be!"

"Yeah, richer is what you'll be. We plan on getting some

of the toys we're donatin' from you. We're comin' over Wednesday night before we see Randy's little girl in the elementary Christmas program. They're a nice little family, and we already knew Carol. She was a cheerleader with our Colleen during high school."

"Small world, huh Harve?"

"I'll say! See ya tomorrow night."

"Hang on, Harve, I've got some news too." Del called out eagerly. The dial tone answered back. Oh well, Harvey could hear about Jean Martin's phone call tomorrow night. Maria's husband had been spotted.

Hometown, 9:00 a.m.

Miss Hawkins, impressed with Suzannah's picture plan, had donated the art paper and granted permission for her to draw in class, as long as it didn't interfere with other work and activities. So between math and recess on Monday Suzannah had sketched. After the program practice, lunch and spelling test, she began drawing as inconspicuously as possible. Before long, though, the word got around about her "special project," and other kids wandered by to take a look.

Someone said, "Wow! Neat idea!"

Someone else said, "Wish I could draw that good."

Gordon Nordan said, "You got the roof all wrong, Miss Teacher's Pet!"

Jordan Nordan said, "Shut up, spaz, and leave her alone."

Suzannah was surprised.

On Tuesday before the first recess, the drawing part was more than halfway finished. During lunchtime people could stay in from the snow if they wanted. Elated, Suzannah continued drawing, full speed ahead.

Someone said, "Groovy color!"

Someone else said, "Far out!"

Gordon Nordan said, "No one would live in a *blue* house!"

Jordan Nordan said, "I told ya to leave her alone!"

"Butt out!"

"Grow up!"

Suzannah was amazed.

Tuesday afternoon she started on the poem. She had

a specific spot for it in the bottom right hand corner of the drawing. It was supposed to be an inspirational poem. Yet words didn't flow as easily for Suzannah as crayon and paint, and she struggled mightily. She wrote ideas on scrap paper, but kept coming up with dumb stuff like:

> Once there was a guy named Randy,
> Who with tools was very handy.
> He wanted to build a new house,
> But his boss was a great big louse.

Of course, that would never work! Although it might be true, it wasn't exactly the sentiment the picture called for. The next poem she wrote started out even worse:

> Someday we'll live in a brand-new house,
> And not give a care if your boss is a louse.

Again, it was unacceptable. Frustrated, she went out for afternoon recess.

"We have to help her!"
Ginny shook her head.
"Why Ginny? This gift is important! Let's get Elizabeth."
"Which Elizabeth?"
"The one I met in the east garden. She told me her prettiest poem, 'How do I love thee, let me count the ways.' That's the kind of words Suzannah needs. Let's get Elizabeth!"
"No, little one. Suzannah must find her own words for this gift. It will work better if she does."
"I don't know ..."
"Trust me."
"Well, if she tries and tries and tries and can't get it right, can we get Elizabeth?"
"We'll see."

Hometown, 2:00 p.m.

After the final bell for afternoon recess rang, Suzannah rushed into the classroom invigorated; ready to give the poem another try. When she reached her desk she gasped in horror. Across the "poem corner" of her picture, someone had scrawled:

> Dad wanted to build a house, it's true.
> But not a barn that's painted blue.
> He said, I'm glad my boss is big old louse,
> It kept me from building this ugly, stinking house.

"Miss Hawkins!" the Suzannah siren sounded.

"Ginny!"
"Hold on! Have faith!" was all Ginny would say.

Miss Hawkins ran for Suzannah. Gordon Nordan ran for cover. Miss Hawkins found tissues and began mopping up Suzannah's tears. Jordan found Gordon hiding out in the utility closet and began some mopping up of his own.

Crack! Crash!

The whole class ran out into the hallway. They stood transfixed, listening to the noises coming from behind the closet door.

"Jerk!"

"Creep!"

Bang! Slap! Whap!

Miss Hawkins spoke firmly, "Boys, stop it this instant and open the door!"

Thump! Thud! Oof! Ugh!

"Idiot!"

"Fink!"

Rip! Bop! Groan!

"Boys, open this door immediately!" Miss Hawkins pounded on the door. "Go back into classroom!" she snapped at the rest of the students,

Nobody moved.

A frightful tremor, like a belly-flopping hippo, smashed against the closet door, shook the floor, and then all was calm.

"Boys?" the teacher called out timidly, her hand trembling over her heart.

A few torturously slow seconds later the closet door opened. Jordan Nordan, his lip puffy, walked stiffly out. The collar of his brown, plaid shirt collar dangled, halfway torn off. With an air of dignity, he ambled back to the classroom. Admiring classmates scattered to let him pass, then followed. Most would have given their twelve-year molars for a chance to knock know-it-all Gordon Nordan around a bit.

Suzannah was smitten. No one had ever defended her so bravely. She was speechless, which suited Jordan just fine because he couldn't even look in her direction. He simply sat down at his desk and put his head down.

Miss Hawkins reached into the utility closet to help Gordon to his feet. He jerked his arm away from her and struggled to stand up unaided. Nose bleeding, two shirt buttons missing, he sported large reddening welts on cheekbone and chin.

"I believe you have something to say to Suzannah," Miss Hawkins chastised, pointing toward the classroom. "March!"

Wiping his bloody nose on his green plaid shirtsleeve, Gordon staggered back into the room. Again the center of attention, he slowly limped up to Suzannah, and said, loud enough for all to hear, "My brother loves you!"

"Why, you little … " Jordan yelled in rage and flew at Gordon again.

Suzannah was in shock.

Hometown, 7:30 p.m.

Before bed as Suzannah painstakingly re-created the gift picture, she marveled at the events of the day. She relived the ordeal of the ruined artwork, the closet fight, and the scene of Miss Hawkins dragging the Nordan boys to the principal's office after the second fight. What kept coming to her mind most was Gordon Nordan's blaring declaration, "My brother loves you!"

Thinking about it gave Suzannah an odd feeling in the pit of her stomach, like being excited and carsick at the same time. Half of her mind screamed: Jordan Nordan? How gross! The other half thought differently. He stood up for her, even whupped his own brother for her sake. Hmm. Imagine that! Suzannah felt so inspired that she wrote the entire "house of dreams" poem in ten minutes.

"She did it, Ginny, she did it!" the little spirit squealed with delight.

"I knew she could."

"How did you know?"

"I knew she had the words in her all along, but too much world-noise kept her from hearing them. That poem is a song from Suzannah's heart. As soon as she found time to be quiet and calm she could feel the music. Your parents will feel it too, and it will mean more to them because it sounds like her."

The spirit child hugged Ginny mightily.

Hometown, 10:00 p.m.

Suzannah sat in bed writing.

"Dear Diary, What a crazy day it's been! I can't even tell you about it all tonight. Got to get to sleep soon. Anyway, I finished Dad's present. What a big relief! Now for the class party and school program, then Christmas break, yea!!

"I've been thinking about dreams and stuff tonight. They come in lots of shapes and sizes. Play dreams like me and Debbie wanting to be movie stars or Miss Americas. Disappointing dreams like Dad's house and a better future that didn't work out. Sad dreams like when Debbie's brother Steve and his buddies went to war to save the day and become big heroes like their dads or grandpas had been. Now Steve is missing in action and one friend is dead.

"It's a horrible world sometimes! I sure wish there was more happiness in it, and sunny days and families that hug a lot and landlords who like dogs. You know my dream … getting a sister. Mom really tried. Having a bunch of kids was her dream. Dang miscarriages! Sometimes I look at all the packed boxes of baby stuff and feel like crying. Mom doesn't talk about it. Now it's probably too late. Dad sleeps on the couch half the time. Not a good sign. I keep praying, though."

Suzannah turned back about twenty pages in her diary. She reread passages of the weird dream she'd had several weeks back. "It wasn't scary, just strange. I was asleep like Sleeping Beauty but not quite. And when I woke up Mom walked in carrying a baby." She used to think it meant something. Now she wasn't sure.

She resumed writing. "Got to go. Good night. Sweet dreams, diary!"

Tuesday night Suzannah dreamed about Jordan Nordan. It wasn't a scary dream, but it wasn't exactly Sleeping Beauty either. It was definitely strange, though, and in the morning she decided not to even tell her diary.

<hr>

"Did you have dreams too, Ginny?"

"I did. Some of them came true, some didn't. Motherhood was one that didn't. I wanted to teach my children many wonderful things. But our son died as a baby and we couldn't have any more. It was one of my biggest life challenges."

"Did you teach him here?"

"Actually, he's taught me, and we talk often about how our family will be reunited, and life challenges will have become blessings."

"But the ones waiting on earth are very sad."

"Enduring sad times now will bring eternal joys. I've seen it. I've lived it. I know."

<hr>

Wednesday, December 22, 1965

Hometown, 2 p.m.

The class bash on Wednesday turned out to be great fun, plenty of chips, brownies, iced sugar cookies and a 2-gallon Tupperware container of Kool-Aid spiked with 7-Up. Suzannah showed her finished picture, which was immediately whisked away to the office by the teacher, mostly for safekeeping, but also to be laminated so it would last forever.

Everyone had a good time, though the day didn't exactly go as planned. The glue mix for the Santa's elf piñata had dried like concrete, so the darn thing couldn't be broken. At first it was funny. After everyone had a turn whacking it with a broomstick it was barely dented

The Nordan brothers, who had been getting along all day and were unusually polite to Miss Hawkins, looked at each other as if mind-reading, then raced toward the equipment corner.

Within seconds each came back sporting a baseball bat, grinning as broadly as their bruised cheeks and swollen lips would allow. They took up spots on opposite sides of the poor piñata.

"Boys, I'm not sure that's such a good ..." Miss Hawkins began to say.

It was too late. With one thunderous whack, both bats hit the Santa's elf at once. It exploded! Sugary shrapnel and colored paper flew in all directions. The classroom erupted into a frenzy, students grabbing for whatever treats they could find. Multicolored gum drops, the only candy not pulverized by the blast, went bouncing and careening every which way, like runaway rainbow rabbits seeking refuge under desks, tables, and chairs. Students turned into ravenous hunters and the noise decibels rose to an unhealthy level.

Miss Hawkins decided to take a coffee break.

The chaos continued with shouts and laughter as each fugitive gumdrop was found. Suzannah had gathered six of them, and was on hands and knees reaching under the S.S.R. bookcase for the seventh, when her hand touched something warm. It *grabbed* her!

She jerked her hand back, gasped in enough air to fill a weather balloon, and was about to utter the shriek of her life, when Jordan Nordan crawled around from the other side, a horrified grimace on his face. The thing had grabbed *him* too.

Time froze as they knelt face to face. Their brains de-frosted as soon as they realized there wasn't a *thing* under the bookcase. They had grabbed each other!

Jordan's face turned crimson.

"Sorry," Suzannah giggled.

Jordan smiled, holding out the gumdrop for her to take.

She was about to thank him when an annoyingly familiar voice inquired, "Ah hah! And what do we have here?"

Jordan's hand snapped back. He jumped up to confront Gordie. "Nothing!" he said, venom in his voice.

"Looks like something."

"Get your eyes checked!"

Suzannah stood, brushed the dust off her skirt and walked away. The last place she wanted to be was between those two. She'd seen what they'd done to the piñata!

Silence hit the classroom in one electric wave. The Nordan boys were keenly aware of the group, including Miss Hawkins, who reappeared in the doorway and stood giving them the evil eye.

"Time to clean up," she said, brusquely, "Clean the area where you are standing, then check by your desk. Move quickly. Begin now!"

The students did as they were told, just more quietly than normal, straining to hear what "the brothers" were saying as they scooped debris into piles awaiting the broom.

Ever keen to an audience, Gordy said, in a fake whisper, "It's okay. Everybody knows you like her."

Through clenched teeth Jordan mumbled, "I do not!"

"Oh, that's right. You don't like her, you ..."

Interrupting, Jordan hissed a warning, "You like your teeth?"

"Yeah."

"You want to wear 'em home, or take 'em in your pocket?"

"Touchy! Touchy!"

"Shut up!"

They came to attention as Miss Hawkins made the rounds, supervising the particle pickup. After she passed by the Nordans and okayed their area, Gordy turned his back so the class couldn't hear. "You don't like her?"

"No!"

"Then prove it!" Gordy said, with a canary-eating grin.

The color drained from Jordan's face.

———

Ginny was distressed by the tone of that comment. "Those boys are up to no good."

"The naughty one is very cute!"

"Cute? He's the one that we need to keep an eye on most!"

"Okay, I will."

Ginny did not like the tone of that comment either. But her thoughts were drawn again to the screen.

———

Mayville, 6:00 p.m.

Harvey and Enid made a trip into Del's store before the Christmas program. It had been a long time since they'd had an excuse to seriously browse through a toy section. Their kids were all grown up. Their youngest daughter, Charlene was in Germany with her husband, who was in the army. She'd been married two years and had a baby due in April. Colleen, who was living in Denver working as a nurse, was dating a doctor. Harve Robert and Patricia had Thomas, age 7, and Tiffany, age 5, whom Enid and Harvey loved dearly, but hadn't been able to be involved with as much as they'd like.

Miss Prim and Mister Proper, Harvey called them privately, because they were so nervous and finicky. Thomas was a real mixture of both parents: his dad's brown hair, his mom's blue eyes. He didn't seem to care for rough-and-tumble activities, was very polite and seemed intelligent enough, but exhibited no trace of enthusiasm unless you were talking about airplanes. Harve Bob and he shared that interest, and his room had several miniatures on display, not with the particular approval of Patricia.

Tiffany, a true miniature of her mother, refused to play outside when they were out at the farm. She hated to get dirty. Her mother had started a Madame Alexander doll collection for her at birth. These lined the shelves of her distinctly decorated bedroom. She was allowed to play with a baby doll named Puddin' but the others were strictly to-look-at toys.

Patricia kindly provided a specialized catalog for her in-laws each year from which to choose appropriate gifts for her children. At first they pretended to lose it and improvised with choices of their own. This didn't sit well with their daughter-in-law so they'd finally relented. Catalog shopping wasn't much fun; fill out an order form, slap on a bow. But this was fun!

Enid's eyes lit right up when she walked into the drugstore's toy section. She gladly selected four dolls. One was "just darling." Another one was "so precious!" and the last two were "as cute as could be!" She chose a variety of coloring books and crayons next. In the meantime, Harvey picked two dump trucks, four cans of Tinkertoys, six Slinkies, and two Cooties and Candyland games. They stacked things neatly on the counter and floor next to the pharmacy cash register.

"Got everything you need?" Del asked.

"Actually, we were thinking about getting something for that little guy staying with Jean Martin. How old did you say he was?"

"Almost three, I think."

Enid headed off again toward the toy department.

Del continued the conversation with Harvey. "Hey, they have a lead on the whereabouts of his dad!"

"Why didn't you tell me?"

"I would have, if you hadn't hung up so fast the other morning."

"Didn't mean to cut ya off. That's real good news."

Enid carried another armload to the register; a Romper Room jack-in-the-box, a teddy bear, some Little Golden books, three pair of socks, even a pair of Keds from Del's closeout bin of summer sneakers. Harvey chuckled, "Looks like we're gonna need a wagon to carry all that stuff in. Might as well get one of those too." He nodded toward the display with assorted sizes of American Flyers.

"Don't worry about it, Harve. I'll throw that in from myself."

"Well, that's real fine of ya, Del. Thanks! I'm gonna need another big favor too."

"You want me to throw in free gift-wrap. Okay you got it. It's the least I can do for such a good cause."

"Gee, thanks! That's not what I was gonna ask for, but it would sure come in handy since we already have to wrap stuff from Bud's Bargain-All. I was thinkin' that since we're gonna be real busy playing Santa on Christmas Eve, we could sure use someone to take this other load over to Jean Martin's."

"Why don't you ask one of your elves?" Del snickered.

"I think I just did."

Del snapped to attention, saluting, "Private Jones, Elf First Class, at your service, Sir!"

The picture faded.

"Are you crying, Ginny?"

"Yes, tears of joy. I truly enjoy seeing people get into the Christmas spirit."

"Especially people you love?"

Ginny nodded.

The spirit child hugged her softly. "Me too!"

They stood together quietly for a while, then the spirit child asked, "What's a school Christmas program?"

Ginny smiled, her eyes twinkling. "A school Christmas program is something you have to experience to fully comprehend." She pointed to the screen.

Hometown, 6:17 p.m.

Carol Brown rubbed a little VO-5 into Suzannah's long brown hair to give it extra body and shine. She carefully brushed the bouncing curls so the bobbypin dents from the brush rollers wouldn't be obvious, then pulled the top back and twisted a rubber band at the base of it. "Pony tail or braid?" she asked.

With earnest contemplation, Suzannah said, "I'd like a curly ponytail and wear my new hot-pink bow, but I don't think it'd be realistic for Mary to wear that color. Maybe we should just braid it, and weave in red and green ribbon."

Carol Brown smiled. "Good decision. Have you decided what dress to wear?"

"Yeah. My pink one. Lots of girls got new dresses for tonight. But I think it's real dumb to get a new dress for a program when it's going to be covered with an old white shirt. Kind of a waste of money, don't you think?"

Carol stopped brushing. "Maybe next year we can waste a little ourselves."

Suzannah saw the pain in her mother's reflection.

Hometown, 7:40 p.m.

Principal Lundy walked across the big stage in the age-worn auditorium. It was time to start. He'd already waited an extra ten minutes so that latecomers (about a third of the crowd) could get seated. As soon as they were settled he asked them all to stand for the pledge of allegiance. He got a kick out of doing that.

It was a packed house. It reminded him of the old days when the school had been home to all twelve grades, and there'd been dances, basketball playoffs and a wide variety of school and community theatrical productions. Back then it was common to see a large turnout. This many people for an elementary program was astounding!

Principal Lundy proceeded, actually relaxed for once. This was partly due to the fact that the five hundred per-plexing pupils had been rehearsing diligently and he had great confidence in them, but mostly it was because he was minutes away from a two-week vacation from every last one of them.

As the house lights dimmed, the glaring balcony spotlight blinded him temporarily. He raised an arm to shield his eyes and hit the microphone with his elbow. A brash metallic squawk caused adults in the audience to groan, and toddlers to whine.

Embarrassed, Principal Lundy hastened to add humor, "Now that I have your attention, I would like to welcome you all out tonight. I just received word that our students are present and accounted for. But before we begin I'd like to acknowledge Mrs. Wray and teachers who worked many long, hard hours to make this evening possible."

A generous round of applause swept across the huge rectangular room. As the clapping ceased, Mr. Lundy continued. "Now without further ado, we'll proceed with tonight's presentation entitled, 'Songs of Celebration.' Thank you all for coming. Have an enjoyable evening!"

A slight ripple of applause followed. The audience lights dimmed. Another high-pitched protest came from the microphone as it was moved off the stage. Mr. Lundy cursed. Few people noticed because two lines of choir kids entered through the back doorway and began the proces-sion down the side aisles leading to the stage.

Wearing an oversized white shirt with a black crepe paper bow tie, each child carried a flashlight topped with an empty toilet paper cylinder that had been painted yellow for the desired candlelight effect. The 5th and 6th grade girls came in first, walking like reverent Christmas brides all the way up to the chairs on risers at the left side of the stage. Their counterparts lumbered down the aisle toward the right side of the stage with the finesse of a farmhand dragging the manure off the bottom of his boots.

Four boys stuck their "candles" up by their chins and made

horrific grimaces, a few others flashed the ceiling in a random flurry like a light show. This example was not entirely lost on the 2nd-, 3rd- and 4th-grade boys, who would have followed suit had they not been given a death-glare warning by Mrs. Wray. Finally came the sweetly innocent 1st graders, whose degree of cuteness brought an abundance of "oohs" and "ahs" from onlookers. These little tykes filled the chairs placed across the floor for the entire length of the old stage. This setup left a tidy square in the center of the stage where the scenes were to be spotlighted.

Mrs. Wray conducted a splendid combination of secular selections topped off with the traditional tunes of stable and star. And—other than having to take the flashlights away from those who would shine into their mouths to make their cheeks light up, demanding the dripping crepe paper spit wads from three blackened 4th-grade mouths, and consoling a 3rd-grade girl who did the bottom bounce after the Bethlehem song when she went to sit down on the bleachers but found no room at the end—everything went as planned. That is until the last song, and the highly touted, most brilliantly lit "Mary" scene in Hometown Elementary history.

Thursday, December 23, 1965

Mayville, 6:45 a.m.

Good Morning, Harvey," Del called loudly into the telephone. "Sorry, I thought you'd be up chompin' at the bit. You awake?"

"Am now. What's going on?" Harvey asked, groggily.

"I was down at the store with Gunn Gunderson. He told me an incredible story. I had to see if it was true."

"Store? Gunderson? Good grief, little Gunn got croup again?"

"Sure does. Anyway, while I was getting the medicine, Gunn said there was some big excitement at the Hometown elementary last night. I called to get the facts."

Harvey was mumbling something to his wife, but soon returned. "Enid says the old Gunderson place doesn't have much insulation. She was visiting there last week and it was colder than an igloo's icebox. Probably why they can't keep that kid well." Harvey yawned, then continued to ramble. "Did you know that when Gunn Jr. was born, they had a big fight because Gunn Sr. wanted to call him Sonofa?"

"Sonofa Gunderson? I never heard it was true, but I'll bet they get tired of hearing that old joke. Dang it, Harvey, that's not why I called. I want to hear about the Christmas program. Quit stalling!"

Harvey began mumbling off the phone again. A few seconds later he was back on the line, chuckling softly, sounding wide awake. "You should have been there, Del! It was the most interestin' program that I've ever been to."

"So, what was the mystery thing that happened? Gunderson was quite worked up about it. Said something about a halo."

"Halo?" Harvey laughed out loud, then promptly lowered his volume a bit for Enid's sake. "Yeah, it appeared at the end of the program, after one of the younger groups, I think they were 3rd-graders ... Yes, Enid says they were 3rd-graders. Anyway, they finished doing a nativity poem in that sign language stuff. Then the auditorium went pitch-dark except for that huge spotlight shining center stage where Suzannah Brown was doing the Mary scene."

"Yeah, and then ...?"

"The kids were singing, 'Silent Night.' Suzannah Brown sat as still as a painting up there, holdin' that doll tender-like. It was a pretty sight. And except for a few whinin' babies, she had everyone's attention. Then, during the last verse ..."

"That's it!" Del blurted, excitedly. "That's what I want to hear about."

"Then why did you interrupt, for cryin' out loud? I was just gettin' to it."

"Sorry. Go on."

"Okay. Now, like I said, Suzannah was sittin' in that spotlight, and boy, was it bright! The next thing we knew this silvery, horizontal thing rose up slowly behind her and stopped about an inch from the top of her head, reflecting like crazy. It was the most amazing thing you ever saw, and Suzannah didn't seem to know it was there. Pretty soon somebody said, "That girl's got a halo," and people leaned forward, staring into the brightness. There was lots of whispering, and some old lady behind me started praying!"

"Well, was it a halo? Gunn Gunderson thought it was."

"To tell ya the truth, Del, I almost believed it myself, for a few seconds. It really looked like one. As the song ended, the darn thing flashed a couple times, then disappeared. Suzannah jerked up straight all of a sudden, and felt the top of her head. Everyone watched to see what she'd do."

"What'd she do? What'd she *do*?"

"She jumped up and ran behind the curtains. The lady behind me said, 'She's sad because she lost her halo.' The lights came on and lots of folks just sat there, but Carol Brown sure dashed behind that stage fast. When we caught up to her, she was hugging her cryin' kid, holding a huge pair of scissors in her hand."

"Scissors?"

"Yup, that's what the shiny halo was; scissors! They found 'em backstage. Talk about a hoax! Whoever did it reached through a slit in those old heavy green curtains and clipped off a piece of Suzannah's hair!"

"What? They cut her hair?"

"Yup, all but the top four inches of that long braid and ribbons—right off the top of her head. That's why she was cryin', not because she lost her halo."

"If that don't beat all," Del was incredulous. "Who did it?"

"No one knows for sure, and they couldn't find the principal to investigate, so they decided to leave it till after the holidays. Suzannah says she has an idea; said somethin' about the Bobbsey Twins from hell, and has sworn off all boys for life! Then when we were leavin' people were starin' at her. We told them that it was a prank. They didn't believe us. Some even reached out to touch her as she walked by."

"Poor kid. What a night! Maybe I should have gone." Del burst out laughing.

Harvey couldn't help joining him. "Yeah, you missed a good one."

"Man, if I'd ever done that, it'd been the woodshed for sure."

"If you'd ever been caught, ya mean!"

They laughed even louder.

Finally Harvey said, "Hey, let me know when the presents are wrapped and I'll swing by to pick them up. By the way, Randy Brown's comin' by to work on the tractor some more today. Suzannah's comin' too. Enid's promised to take her over to Hannah's Hair Hut and get that top part of her hair trimmed up somehow."

"Okay, Harve. Talk to you later. I still can't believe it!"

"See what you miss when you work too hard?" Harvey teased.

"Spoken like a true hypocrite!" Del returned the jest.

"Those stinkers!" Ginny said, recalling the school program.

"Father's Messenger told those boys to stop. Why didn't they listen?"

"They chose not to."

"Will they get in trouble?"

"Probably not enough to learn from this experience. Some choices we learn from immediately. Other choices have delayed consequences or painful lessons that require making amends before progress or healing begins."

"Is it hard to make good choices?"

"Not as hard if you ask Father for guidance, then listen closely."

The spirit child pondered this, and then asked, "Why did people want to believe in the halo?"

"Because deep in their souls they miss Father's kingdom, and what they saw awakened those feelings. Most want to believe in heaven, then start to doubt the possibility. But we're closer than they think, aren't we?"

The child touched the edge of the shimmering screen with awe. "Yes, we are. It's sad they can't remember."

"They'd get too homesick if they did. Earth life is a difficult schooling experience and they need to concentrate on their homework." Ginny smiled. "In the meantime we watch over them all."

"Even the naughty ones."

"Even the naughty ones. We send the light but don't force them out of the darkness. They have to choose, or the change has no power. That was decided a long time ago and everyone agreed."

"Are Del and Harvey still nice? They laughed about Suzannah."

"They're still nice. They laughed because what happened was outrageous, and because they remember being mischievous boys themselves. Suzannah wasn't actually hurt and someday she may laugh about it too. One thing's for sure, this is one Christmas program she'll never forget!"

"Poor Suzannah! Why don't those boys like her?"

"I'd say one of them likes her very much."

"The tall one?"

"Yes, the tall one. The other one …"

"Is really cute!"

"Yes, but he's a rascal, taking advantage of a situation to give his brother a difficult time. That's not a nice thing to do."

"I hope they hurry and make amends, I like the cute one!"

Ginny's eyes opened wide in alarm. She quickly changed the subject. "It's Christmas Eve down there now. It might be fun to watch, or we could stop for a while if you'd like."

"No, we should check in on them, since we're waiting to see Christmas anyway."

Ginny smiled. "Then checking in, it is!"

Friday, December 24, 1965

The City. 6:30 p.m.

Patricia Watterson and her roast turkey entourage showed up at the Hope for Life Center at 6:30 p.m. as planned. Her group included several family friends from the community: a land developer (her husband), a prominent banker, a respected dentist, and the Deputy Mayor, (family friends, each with corresponding spouse.) Everything was thoroughly organized, and a complete dinner along with dessert was served to eighty-two people in less than two hours, including cleanup. Each adult received a neatly wrapped bundle that held a pair of gloves, a stocking hat, a toothbrush, a five-dollar bill and a map of The City. The children had to wait for Santa, who, Patricia assured them, was due right on schedule. At precisely 8:15 p.m. her group was packed up and out the door.

Santa casually drove up at 8:35; driving an old Chevy pickup with a big pile of presents neatly stacked under a heavy, green tarp in the back. Mrs. Santa was there too, wearing a ruffled holiday apron over a long red dress, eager to help hand out her traditional Christmas cookies with holiday sprinkles to thirty-seven of the most surprised and appreciative youngsters that the two had ever seen.

Mayville, 9:30 p.m.

Jean Martin's house was visited by a mysterious elf who left a gift-filled wagon on the doorstep for little Carlos and a large wrapped box of well-kept used clothing, including a brand-new coat for Maria.

By coincidence of course, Del Jones showed up a bit later to drop off a purple-ribboned box of Maxfield's chocolates, and a festive jar filled with Brach's Christmas candy. He was invited to stay for hot cider and some of Jean's famous cinnybuns. He was still there when a call came from San Vega.

"A ...a, is Jean Martin there?" the deep voice asked, hesitantly.

"This is Jean."

"Um ... This is Jake Boyer again, and I ..."

Jean interrupted, "Yes, Jake. Good to hear from you. Any luck yet?"

"No. That's what I called about, ma'am. I know I saw that guy the other day, but honestly, I can't locate him now. I'm real sorry. I know how much you wanted to hear good news, especially on Christmas Eve, and I did try, Miss Martin."

"I'm sure you did, Jake. Don't worry about it. We appreciate what you've done."

"You're welcome, I just wish ... well, anyway I'll try again on Sunday. I swear it's like he's hiding or something. None of his friends seem to know his whereabouts."

"Hmmm," Jean responded. "Mr. Boyer, it's possible that he doesn't know he can trust you, and his friends are protecting him."

"Yeah, I thought about that, but what can I do?"

"I'm not sure. Give me your number. I'll talk to his wife and we'll call you back." Jean wrote down the number, said, "Thanks again. We'll get back to you in a bit."

Hometown, 10:35 p.m.

"Time for bed, Suz," Carol Brown called through her daughter's bedroom door.

"Okay, Mom. I'm almost done. Be out in a minute." She hadn't anticipated how difficult it would be to wrap Dad's picture. It was so thin. If she wrapped it flat, he'd guess it was a picture right away. She couldn't roll it, of course, because it was laminated. After sitting like a listless lump for half an hour, she had finally decided to wrap it several times to make it at least look thicker.

The first layer was tissue paper. Next came three double layers of newspaper, each taped down hard, followed by two different kinds of Christmas wrapping paper. She had just finished the ribbon when her mom knocked on her door.

What a day it had been! She'd spent the morning trying to style her new hairdo; a long shag, the beautician had called it. After that, she'd gone sledding and tubing for several hours up Hiddencove Canyon with her friend Debbie. Even later, she'd helped deliver cookies and her mom's famous hand-dipped chocolates to their friends and neighbors, even to their grumpy landlord, Mr. Metzler.

Exhausted, she'd dozed off during the Jimmy Stewart movie about the guy and the angel. She looked so peaceful on the couch that her parents were tempted to let her sleep there all night and tiptoe off to bed, when Bam! Bam! Bam! A harsh knock shook the front door. Suzannah jerked awake and her mom went to see who it was.

No one was there.

A grocery bag was sitting in the snow on the porch. In it were two presents and a small hand-printed note that read: "For Suzannah."

One of the presents looked like it came from Denton's Five and Dime and smelled suspiciously like cherry chocolates. The other was a weird oblong gift, which felt soft and squishy.

"I wonder who left it?" her dad said.

Her mom shrugged, expecting Suzannah to pester them as usual about opening the gifts immediately. Suzannah didn't have time to be a slave to suspense tonight. She still had Dad's present to wrap!

"I guess we'll have to find out in the morning," she said, on the way to her room with all the wrap, ribbon and tape she could find.

"Who was that stranger?" Carol Brown asked her husband in amazement after Suzannah was gone.

"I don't know. Do you suppose they switched kids on us at the beauty parlor?"

San Vega, 11:15 p.m.

The telephone rang at the Boyer home.

"Hello."

"Hi, Jake. This is Jean Martin again. After talking with

Maria, we think we've got the perfect message for you to give to her husband if you see him. Sort of like a password. One that he'll know came directly from her."

"Okay. Hold on while I get something to write on." Jake searched the nightstand drawer for paper and pen. He settled for the back of the church flyer that he'd tucked away for safekeeping, and a blue colored pencil he found on the floor.

"Go ahead," he said, listening intently.

"Now write it the way it sounds so you can pronounce it correctly."

"Gotcha!"

When Jean finished relaying the message, he asked, "You really think this will do the trick?"

"If *that* doesn't do it, *nothing* will! Thanks again for trying, Jake. Merry Christmas to you and your family."

"And to you too, Miss Martin. Bye."

"Who was that?" his wife, Connie asked, coming into the bedroom from the bathroom, where she'd slipped into Jake's favorite present; a cute little Christmas nightie.

"It's some words I'm supposed to say to that Sanchez guy when I find him, so he'll know that I'm on an errand from his wife and he can trust me."

Looking at the words on the paper, Connie raised an eyebrow and asked, "And you're sure this message will work?"

Jake reached out and pulled her toward him. With a sly grin, he said, "I don't know if that message will work, but the one you're sending sure does."

"Hold on a minute," Connie giggled. She stood on the bed so she could look at him eye to eye, then held a sprig of mistletoe above his head.

The City, 11:20 p.m.

Santa and his wife left very tired from their romp with the kids. The children waved, calling boisterous good-byes. And they heard him exclaim ere he drove out of sight, "Giddy-up, Blue. Time to go home and wake up the reindeer!"

Saturday, December 25, 1965

*M*erry Christmas, little one!"
"*Merry Christmas to you too, Ginny. It's a big day for me and my family.*"
"*And for many others. Good luck!*"
"*What's luck?*"
"*On earth it's a word that means a surprise blessing.*"

Hometown, 8:20 a.m.

"Wake up, sleepyhead!" Randy Brown said, shaking the bottom of Suzannah's bed slightly. "It's almost 8:30! You've never slept this late on Christmas. Debbie's called twice since six to see what you got."

Suzannah jumped out of bed and raced to the living room. The first present was a comfy, red rosebud flannel nightgown that her mom had made. She got two 45 rpm records: The Beach Boys "The Little Girl I Once Knew" and "Mrs. Brown You've Got A Lovely Daughter" by Herman's Hermits and "The Sound of Music" album. There was a heart pendant necklace, two pairs of tights, an Avon bubble bath and mint-flavored lip-gloss.

A fluorescent-purple plastic case had been left by Suzannah's newly acquired "Auntie Enid" and contained a large set of pink spongy rollers, two headbands, three cards of barrettes, and a hairbrush with a tortoise-shell handle. A little note said simply, "to help with the new hairdo."

The last gift box held a floppy-eared, droopy-eyed hound dog that Suzannah could sprawl out on her bed, with a zipper in its brisket where she could keep her folded pajamas if she wanted to.

"That will have to do till we can get the real thing," Mom said.

"Thanks a lot, you guys!" Suzannah said and gave them each a hug. "Now it's time for your gifts. Mom should open hers first."

Carol Brown untied the ribbon, and peeked inside the wrapping.

"Wow, thanks!" She appeared sweetly bewildered. "Look. Suz gave me perfume."

"You can wear it for Dad. I'll bet he'd like that," Suzannah whispered conspiratorially.

Carol's eyes widened. "*Would* you like that, *honey?*"

Randy started to blush. "Of course, *dear.*"

Suzannah ignored their sarcasm. "Okay, Dad, your turn."

"I can't for the life of me figure out what it is. It's the size of a cookie sheet, but weighs less than a cookie!"

"Open it!"

"Okay, here goes." Agonizingly slow he began to tear through layer upon layer, hamming it up like he was dying of suspense, which sent Suzannah and even her mom into fits of laughter. Finally, he looked at the picture and read the poem out loud, or at least tried:

> "One day we'll live in our house of dreams,
> Where Dad is king and Mom is queen.
> We'll laugh and sing and dance all day,
> And never let grumpiness get in our way.
> We'll be cozy in winter, spring, summer and fog,
> And be so happy we'll get a dog.
> Each night the king will say to his wife,
> This is a wonderfully marvelous life!"

Randy cleared his throat several times. Carol leaned over his shoulder and finished reading:

> "P.S. Don't give up your dreams, Dad, or start to fret,
> 'Cause the ones coming up are the best ones yet!"

He gazed down proudly at his laminated treasure.

Suzannah was worried. "Don't you like it?"

"He likes it, honey. We both do," her mom said, tears filling her eyes. "We'll get a beautiful frame for it, won't we?"

"Sure will!" Randy said, his voice finally clear.

"Merry Christmas!" Suzannah said, as she hugged each of them separately, then pulled them together for a group hug.

A few minutes later, when her mom went to get tissues, her dad cleared his throat again, and said, "There is one part of that poem I'm curious about."

"What's that?"

Rubbing his chin like a heavy thinker, he asked, "Just when were the seasons changed to winter, spring, summer, fog?"

Suzannah's face turned bright pink. "When I needed a rhyme for dog!"

Hysterical laughter greeted Carol when she returned with the Kleenex. "It's a good thing that I brought the whole box!" she added, picking up the picture again. "Maybe we should consider painting our new house blue. It looks so neat that way in the picture."

"Maybe we should consider those last two presents," Randy said, pointing to the anonymous gifts under the tree.

"Yes, let's solve that mystery," her mom said, handing Suzannah the packages.

Suzannah tore the Christmas wrap off the large square one first. "Cherry chocolates like I thought. Sorry, Dad, none for you."

"You're right. Don't want a Christmas rash. But since you've already got your dessert, I get dibs on your share of the frosted sugar cookies!"

"In your dreams!" Suzannah laughed, tearing open the weird rectangular gift. She gasped! There in the ripped wrapping was Suzannah's missing braid!

"I don't believe it," her mom said, incredulously.

Their attention was drawn to the green ribbon that was still tied to the hair. On the dangling end of the ribbon someone had written: "Sorry!"

"See, it was a prank, and the prankster felt guilty and decided to repent."

"I don't think it's true repentance," Suzannah scoffed.

"Why not?" both parents asked at once.

"Because whoever gave it back, kept the red ribbon!"

⁂

"Is everything all better now?"

"It's not all better, but they've got a good start."

"Did they find their divine spark?"

"They saw a glimmer of it. Restoring the spark will take time and effort. Keeping it alive may be one of their Life Challenges."

"This has to work, Ginny. It just has to!"

"In the meantime, we'll wait, watch and ..."

"... hope, hope, hope, hope!"

⁂

Mayville, 10:30 a.m.

Maria's little Carlos ran wildly around Jean Martin's living room, tossing Christmas wrapping with delirious delight. He would stop every few minutes, pick up a new toy or one of Maria's new boots, give it a hug, then race around again. Maria shook her head and smiled. She was wearing a lovely outfit from the box the elf had left and holding the new coat on her lap admiring its workmanship.

Jean recognized the items as having once been Virginia's and knew how difficult it must have been for Del to remove them from her closet at last, let alone to give them to another. Jean was very proud of him, and knew Virginia would have been, too. She made sure to take lots of photos with her little Instamatic so the joy in that room could be captured and shared at another time.

Grabbing the embroidered hand puppet his mother had made, Carlos brought it to Jean and said, "Again!"

Jean put it on her hand, and began saying things like, "Merry Christmas, Carlos! Are you a happy boy?" "You sure are a good boy!" and so on, and so on, until he squealed and galloped about again.

"Your present is wonderful," Jean said, turning to Maria. "I can tell it is his favorite one!"

Maria looked very pleased.

Jean brought out the handkerchief that Maria had given to her. Lovingly, she traced the beautiful, elaborate stitching, running her finger along the circles of petite flowers and the letters "J M" in the center of the cloth. She reached out to give Maria's hand a loving squeeze, "Gracias, mi amiga, esta muy bonito!"

Tears flowed as they hugged in gratitude.

Hometown, 1:47 p.m.

Del Jones arrived at the Watterson's half an hour early with a gallon of Cream o'Valley Vanilla Ice Cream.

"See you've come prepared," Harvey teased.

"Absolutely! We can't have bare pie running' around. Besides, it's the only thing that wife of yours hadn't already bought or made. A fella's gotta feel useful, ya know."

"It'll be appreciated. Take your coat off and make yourself at home. The kids will be here in a few minutes."

At 2:20, Robert and his family arrived. Enid made a spectacular fuss over Patricia's beautiful blue fox fur jacket, and Patricia appreciated every minute of it.

Harvey admired it too, but with less finesse. "Heck, if I'd known how much you like fur, I have a whole barn full of cats I would have skinned for ya," he said, holding out a hanger.

Robert beat a path to the safety of the kitchen.

Reluctantly, Patricia took the jacket off so it could be hung up. "Well, this way the cats are safe!" she muttered when Harvey stepped away.

"Have a nice Christmas?" Del Jones asked, politely.

"Yes, it was lovely, with so many nice things. My favorite, after my jacket, naturally, was a night course that my precious husband signed me up for at the university called, 'The Essence of the Poem.' I'm ecstatic!"

"Well, don't worry, you'll do fine," Del said, then hurried off to find Harvey.

"Psst! Patricia! Come here," Robert beckoned from the kitchen as soon as Enid left for a moment to talk to the children. Curious, Patricia quickly went through the swinging doors.

"What is it?"

Robert smiled. "I thought you'd like to see what Dad gave Mom."

"A blender and a box of chocolates, like every year. Right?"

"Wrong. This year he gave her a waffle iron and chocolates."

"What a clever idea," Patricia smiled sarcastically.

"Yeah, it was! Take a look inside."

"If you insist." She lifted the top of the new waffle iron to humor her husband. There inside was a pretty Christmas card, two airline tickets to Hawaii, and a $300 check so Enid could buy "the cutest grass skirt she could find."

"They're going for Valentine's Day. So, what do you think about old, boring Harvey now?"

Patricia fluttered her eyelashes. "I'm tremendously pleased to see that my good taste has finally had a positive influence on this family."

Robert's mouth dropped wide open in amazement. Patricia grabbed a cookie from the cookie tray, stuffed it into his mouth, and ran giggling into the living room.

"Christmas is so different on earth!" the little spirit mused.

"Yes, sometimes they get carried away. But when they genuinely give and share, they add a hint of heaven to the chaos."

"The first Christmas was the best, wasn't it Ginny?"

"The very best one! Remember when it was time for Jesus to go to earth, and everyone gathered to see Him leave?"

"It was so quiet!"

"Remember, when Father gave Jesus His Life Challenges, how Father wept?"

"Because it was such a hard thing Jesus had to go do."

"And Jesus looked at all of us around Him …"

"Like He loved us so much!"

"And He said, 'Yes, I accept.'

The spirit child nodded. "I waved good-bye to Him."

"I think everyone did."

"Even Father."

"And the music was sublime!"

"The most beautiful songs we've ever heard! And we felt so wonderful that we thought we would POP! And everyone hugged and wanted to feel that way forever."

"Yes." Ginny smiled then shook her head. "Unfortunately, on earth, it's easy to forget that Jesus is the reason for Christmas."

"I hope I remember," the spirit child sighed, thoughtfully.

Sunday, December 26, 1965

San Vega, 5:45 a.m.

Jake Boyer woke up before his alarm went off. He hadn't slept all night. It might have been the ghost of Christmas dinner coming back to haunt him. He'd had baked ham, potato salad, rolls, whipped cream fruit salad, pumpkin pie and an assortment of Christmas candy. Before bed, he'd had another slice of pie topped with more whipped cream fruit salad. That was the reason for the insomnia he told himself, but knew there was more to it.

It was a wondrous thing to see little Ronnie yesterday ride like a ruffian on his new Wonder Horse, terrorize the Christmas tree with his Tonka truck, or try to figure out how his new toy barn full of plastic animals said, "Moo" when the door was opened. Jake couldn't help wondering how Eduardo Sanchez was feeling.

It bothered Jake that the guy who'd kept him from spending his holiday in the hospital was missing out on Christmas with his own kid; not knowing how, or where he was. If it was me, Jake thought, I'd be going nuts! His stomach grumbled in agreement. He had a Pepto Bismol breakfast, then headed for work.

The stores on the Saturday run had been closed for Christmas but would be expecting deliveries today. The short run had to be completed a.s.a.p., and the truck reloaded for the usual Sunday-Thursday trip. Steve showed up for work a little early for once; still there was no sign of Eduardo, so they loaded up and left. Returning after 1:00, they began the process again. Jake marked things off as they were loaded. Potatoes, tomatoes, apples. Check! Lemons, limes, oranges. Check!

A strange feeling came over Jake. He hesitated, looking around. Nothing was wrong. He resumed the count. While checking the limes, he just happened to glance sideways. That's when he saw the familiar figure in the red shirt, cowering behind the orange crates. Bingo!

Slowly, Jake reached into his shirt and brought out the "Please help me find my Daddy" flyer that he'd picked up from the church and had later copied Maria's message onto. He looked up, smiled at Eduardo and said, in English, loud enough to be heard. "All the stars shine in your eyes and lead me to heaven."

Three men from other delivery companies who were standing nearby looked astonished at Jake. Eduardo's face filled with panic. He began looking around for a better place to hide. He had no idea what the big guy had said, but that smile was spooky! He started to run.

"No! Wait!" Jake yelled, running after him. "All the stars shine in your eyes and lead me to heaven!" he repeated, again in English. Several other men, who had been talking in a group, began to listen to Jake instead. Eduardo ran.

Jake ran too, calling out, "All the stars... Hey, you idiot. I'm trying to tell ya something!"

"Say it in Spanish, lover-boy," someone hollered, making kissing noises. Someone else whistled. Jake was ready to go find those suckers and let 'em kiss his knuckles. But he had a message to deliver, and by heck …

Finally Eduardo ran into a section where the escape route was temporarily blocked by stacked boxes of grapefruit. Jake caught up with him there. Wheezing, he finally tried to deliver the message phonetically, in Spanish. "Todas las estrellas brillan en tus ojos y me llevan al cielo."

Eduardo stopped and turned, staring in disbelief at the paper Jake held.

Jake started repeating the message phonetically again, but before he could finish Eduardo walked forward, took the flyer from Jake and stared at the picture of his son. He started to weep. He hadn't seen the picture since his wallet had been stolen three months earlier, and along with it the only link he had to his wife: Jean Martin's address.

Sid came running up. "What's going on here?"

"Tell this guy that I know where his wife and son are, and that he should come with me to the telephone right now."

"Telephone? What are you talking about?"

Jake looked old Sid straight in the eye and yelled, "Just *do* it!"

Mayville, 2:20 p.m.

Jean Martin walked into her house after visiting a neighbor. She could hear Maria talking, laughing, and crying, all at the same time and was relieved to see that she was on the telephone. Seeing Jean, Maria called out, "Jean, Jean, venga rapido! Lo encontraron! Lo encontraron! He is found! He is found!"

Mayville, 4:00 p.m.

"Hello, Del. This is Jean. Missed you at church today."

"Had to work, after-Christmas sales, you know."

"Yes, I finally realized that after I'd called half a dozen times and no one answered."

"So, what do you need?"

"Did you get your car back yet?"

"Yes, finally. Why?"

Jean hesitated, "It looks like I need to collect that favor you owe me. Maria's husband called today. Jake Boyer's going to bring him to Findley's Fine Foods in Cedar Pines on Wednesday. We're supposed to meet them around five o'clock. It would be a long, stressful bus ride for little Carlos."

"You're not taking the bus. I'll drive you."

"Thanks," she said, her voice shaking.

"Are you okay, Jean?"

"I'm gonna be. Talk to you later."

"Oh, Ginny! Connections are so wonderful!"

"Yes, especially when they turn out well."

"I'm happy for Maria, but poor Jean will be awfully lonely again!"

"Yes, at first. Jean will fill in the loneliness by helping someone else. She's become an expert at soothing solitary souls."

"Will it be someone special?"

"Very special indeed and she's already begun. She just doesn't know it yet!"

The Following Year

San Vega, Wednesday, January 5, 1966

Boyer Brothers, Inc., hired Eduardo Sanchez to work as their dock supervisor and assistant deliveryman. By March 22nd, their business had increased enough that they bought another truck. On May 22nd, Connie announced to Jake that she was pregnant again, and on May 23rd, Jake proudly told everyone the good news as he shook hands as the best man at his brother Steve's wedding.

San Vega, Sunday, June 12, 1966

Maria and Eduardo became the proud parents of a beautiful baby girl. They named her Alicia Jean Martina Sanchez.

Mayville, Thursday, July 21, 1966

Jean Martin sold the little house on the corner of Ash and Oak and made plans to move into The City in a two-bedroom apartment near Children's Hospital, where she had recently been appointed *Head of Volunteer Services*. Later that week she bought a new car; a Rambler Classic, and could actually drive it! Thanks to the driving lessons she'd been receiving each Sunday afternoon since the end of May, when Del Jones had started coming over for dinner.

Hometown, Wednesday, August 10, 1966

Harvey and Enid Watterson left to serve on a two-year Christian mission in South America for their church. Two days later, Suzannah Brown and her parents moved into the Watterson's home to take care of it while they were gone. This helped the family save a hefty down payment for their new house, which was to be the first one built in Rosewood Estates.

Randy Brown, who had been back to work at the mine since March quit August 26th to become the new chief mechanic at Moyd's Motors.

Hometown, Thursday, September 1, 1966

Happy 13th Birthday, Suzannah Brown!

That morning at breakfast, Carol Brown came across an interesting ad in the classified section of the *Hometown Harbinger*, which read:

"Free puppies. Mom is a purebred. Dad is a mystery. Help!"

"What will you name him, Suz?"

Delicately holding the furry brown-black bundle in both hands, Suzannah said, "Maybe Tiny!"

"How about Muttsy, due to his great heritage?" Randy Brown offered.

"Dad!" Suzannah protested. "Its not *his* fault!"

Holding up one of the genetically-destined huge puppy paws, Carol Brown said, "Tiny, huh? That'll last about three months! After that we'll be calling him Pest and yelling at him to quit tromping down the flower beds!"

"Maybe we should call him Tromper to begin with," Randy suggested.

"That's it!" Suzannah squealed. "Tromper Muttsy Brown!"

Suzannah's mom cracked up laughing. "Thought he took after your side of the family!" she teased her husband.

He answered, "Woof, woof!"

The City, Thursday, September 1, 1966

At Bachman's downtown store, tickets went on sale at $100 per couple, for the first annual Christmas Charity Ball to be held in the rotunda of the State Capital Building. It was sponsored by a new, extremely influential women's service club called the *Christmas Belles*, and featured Patricia Watterson as club president.

All in all, it was an exceptionally good year ...until ...

Hometown, 8:46 p.m. Monday, October 31, 1966

Suzannah and her friend Debbie stopped to listen before crossing the road. Even over the racket of Halloween revelers, they could hear the souped-up '57 Chevy coming. "Let's wait," Debbie said, cautiously.

Suzannah nodded in agreement. Then she saw little Nellie Nordan wave and start across the road to join her. "No, Nellie, no!" she screamed.

Nellie couldn't hear. The roar of the speeding car two blocks away drowned out the warning. Nellie kept walking. Suzannah ran!

The spirit child stared aghast at the caption and the picture on the screen. "No, Ginny! This is wrong!" the spirit child implored. "Why did this happen? Why?"

Even Ginny was stunned. "I don't know, little one. Suzannah was trying to be helpful, but the driver was going too fast. He'd been drinking and couldn't slow down in time."

"Suzannah's not going to die, is she?"

"I don't think so, but I'll see what I can find out. I'll be right back."

The City, 8:15 a.m. Tuesday, November 1, 1966

The fact that Suzannah Brown survived the surgery that was required to relieve pressure on her swollen brain and set her broken pelvis and shattered leg was a miracle in itself, according to the doctors at Children's Hospital. She had stopped breathing twice during the procedure. Doctors gave guarded words of encouragement to her devastated parents She lay in Intensive Care in a coma beyond their reach.

Electroencephalogram, severe brain contusion, possible brain damage—these words became Carol Brown's least favorite to hear. Within a week she had quit her job, and started riding the bus into The City so she could spend every day at the hospital with her daughter.

Randy drove in each night after work to visit Suzannah and give Carol a ride home. Together they pleaded in prayer. Together they shared comfort and support. Together ... somewhere they would not have been without the efforts of this girl, their precious child, who had reminded them what together was all about.

Heaven's halls echoed with other prayers being sent on Suzannah's behalf.

Get well cards arrived for her at the hospital every day. Phone calls from friends and family were a break from the monotonous waiting, but Carol had little new information to relay. Finally on November eleventh when Suzannah's status was upgraded to critical but stable, the Brown family discovered a new friend.

Jean Martin brought in a beautiful white teddy bear someone had dropped off for Suzannah at the Volunteer Desk.

Carol gasped, noticing an all-too-familiar red Christmas ribbon tied around its neck. With tear-filled eyes she shared its meaning with Jean.

"I heard about that halo incident from a pal of mine, Del Jones."

"So you're Del's Jean? I'm glad to finally meet you. He's told us that you're the neatest lady alive, and that you'd take good care of us here. I think he's your number one fan," Carol teased.

"Well, he's right about one thing, if you need anything; a place to stay, someone to talk to or to help you chew out the doctors, here's my number. Feel free to call anytime."

"Thanks. It's good to have a lifeline. No telling how long we will be here," Carol said, as she placed the teddy bear on the bed near Suzannah. "She's such a great kid, ya know, an angel compared to some I've heard about. She pushed another child from the path of a speeding car ... they almost made it! There were skid marks 75 feet long! Stupid idiot's in jail now. Luckily when his brakes locked up, the car slid sideways before knocking her down. Head-on she would have been killed outright." Carol swallowed hard. "The other little girl got a broken arm, smashed glasses, and some bad bruises. They almost made it across, just needed a few more steps ..." Her voice trailed off into tears. "Do you think God will take her because she's ... so good?"

Jean wrapped an arm around Carol and let her cry. Several minutes later they began talking again. Carol smoothed Suzannah's nightgown and blankets. There wasn't really much she could do. "She'd have a fit if she could see these tubes, this brace contraption, and knew they'd shaved most of her hair off."

"Tell her! Maybe she'll get mad enough to fight back."

"I'll give anything a try," Carol said, patting her daughter's hand. "Thanks again, Jean. I'll tell Del that we've finally met and that he's right about what a great person you are."

"I think he's okay too. Just don't tell him I said so. I'm still playing hard to get!"

The Visit

Ginny returned to the Viewing Place.

"It's been a long time for them," the little spirit empathized.

"Yes, several weeks, and on earth that can feel unbearable."

"Jean tells Suzannah every day to fight for life. Not to give up."

"I'm not surprised. Bless her heart, she used to do the same for me."

"That's terrible!" The spirit child looked stricken.

"Why?"

"Because you died!"

Ginny knelt down to comfort her. "That's not going to happen to your sister for a long time. I know that for certain now. Her eyes flashed. "Another thing I know for certain is that it's time for your interview, little one!" She stood up and held out her hand.

"Time to go? But, but I have to send them my message. Suzannah can't do it now. I need to tell them!"

Ginny paused. "There may still be a way. Come along."

The spirit child somberly took ahold of Ginny's hand. They walked down the azure-tiled hallway, and once again passed through the building's pillared entrance. A fragrant breeze blew across the marbled courtyard.

"I'm going to miss all of this. And you!" The spirit child turned, burying her face in the soft, flowing robe.

"Would you rather stay?"

"And miss Life? Oh no, Ginny. There's too much to do, come on! Let's walk faster, okay? Can you skip?"

Down the pearl-pebble path they skipped until a short distance from the eastern gate. Ginny stopped to pick an iridescent orchid. "Take this to Him, little one."

The spirit child nodded; too excited to speak. They entered the crystalline courtyard. Hallowed harmonies resonated throughout, and tickled the fibers of her being. They were finally singing for her! She crossed the rainbow-flecked floor and knelt before His throne.

His tender smile wrapped around her soul with overpowering warmth. Enraptured, she was beckoned to His side. Lovingly, He drew her near.

"Are you ready, little one?" He asked.

"Yes, Father!"

"Very well. You are being sent to a time, place and family where you will be able to grow in strength and wisdom. You may have blessings that others do not have. Therefore, strive to ease burdens. There will be obstacles; some great, some small. However, you will not be overcome if you humbly ask for direction.

"Truth will strike a chord within your heart and you will seek after it. Share the truths and knowledge you receive. You will recognize my love in small wonders and beautiful sounds. Never doubt it. We await your joyful return. Be valiant, daughter!"

Having said this, He whispered her Life Challenges into her ear. She nodded exuberantly, which pleased Him. He kissed her forehead, and returned her once more to Ginny.

Beaming, she stepped in that direction, then looked down at the orchid in her hand. She gasped, recalling the request. Hoping it wasn't too late; she rushed back to His side, gave Him the flower and whispered earnestly into His ear. He looked deeply into her eyes, then smiled. "Yes, you may."

She engulfed Him for one last hug. "Thank you so much! I will never forget how much You love me!"

"Don't worry, my child, even if you do, I will be here anytime that you need a reminder!"

Ginny waved good-bye as this remarkable child disappeared down the golden staircase that led to the Crossing Corridor. She returned to the viewing place to wait, watch and hope.

Familiar faces began to reappear.

The City, 7:00 p.m. December 3, 1966

Randy Brown arrived at the hospital as usual. He wished today like he did every day for a miracle. His entire being ached for encouraging news. Yet, as soon as he walked into his daughter's hospital room and saw his wife's pale, tired face, he knew that nothing had changed.

Carol came over for a hug. He could sense an extra tightness within her muscles right away, so as gently as he could with his rough mechanic's hands he began to massage the center of her back.

"Ooh, that feels good!" she groaned appreciatively.

"Tough day, huh?"

"About the same. I fell asleep in the chair earlier and now I feel all knotted up." She moved her head slowly from side to side as her husband gently rubbed her neck.

"Why don't you go to the cafeteria, hon? Take a break."

"Yeah, I'm ready for one," Carol sighed, reaching down to get her purse from under the chair next to Suzannah's bed. "Call for me if …"

"Yeah, I know," Randy smiled assuringly, "if anything happens, I'll have you paged immediately!"

Carol kissed him on the cheek and left. Randy sat down by the bed to talk to his comatose girl. "How ya doing today, ZannahSu?" he asked, gently stroking Suzannah's forehead, smoothing the strands of her hair that were fighting to make a comeback. A knot tightened in his stomach and rolled up into his chest. He fought back a suffocating sob for his child's sake. Gotta have faith! Can't give up hope, he mentally scolded himself, and cleared his throat several times before speaking again.

"I rebuilt the engine of an Oldsmobile today. Then at lunch I bought your mom this great poinsettia plant. She wants to wait until you're home to get a tree this year, and that's okay with me. So what do you say? About ready to junk this joint and come home and string popcorn?" Randy longingly gazed at Suzannah's still form.

"That your girl?" a little voice asked.

"What?" Randy looked up, startled. In the doorway stood an angelic little character, about three or four years old, he guessed.

"Is that your girl?" the child asked again.

Randy nodded. "She was hurt very badly. She's sleeping until her head gets better."

The diminutive visitor's luminous eyes reflected serious concern. She nodded and moved slowly around the opposite side of the bed until she was as close to Suzannah as her small stature would allow.

"Her name is Suzannah. Are you a doctor here?" he kidded.

The bright eyes flashed mischievously. "You're a silly daddy!"

"Yeah, I've been told that before," Randy stood up and walked to the small window, fighting back tears again. Good grief man, he mentally chided himself again. You're an emotional wreck! It was hard not to be. Every day brought reminders of Christmas the year before. The laughter, the fun, and the memorable gifts. Holidays meant so much to Suzannah. It broke his heart to think of everyone else celebrating this year when she couldn't.

A rustling noise turned his attention back to his guest. She was perched in the chair next to the bed, practically hovering over Suzannah. Nosy little thing! he thought, yet was intrigued and actually enjoyed the company. The room was too quiet and lifeless otherwise, his poor daughter too inanimate to seem real.

This little sprite was certainly full of life though! Where did she come from, he wondered? She didn't look the slightest bit sick, yet with that fluffy white nightgown and tiny shiny slippers, she must be a patient. "You'd better get down now." He reached out to lift her down. She shook her head adamantly and shrunk from his grasp, her eyes returning their intensified gaze to Suzannah's face.

Randy decided that since she wasn't hurting Suzannah, he would let her be near a little longer. "Are you lost? Is your mommy around here? I could help you find your mommy. What's your name?"

She studied him a moment. "Suzannah was supposed to tell you," she said, matter-of-factly, yet not blaming.

"Well, she hasn't been talking much lately. You could tell me and I'll remind her when she wakes up. Is it Janey?"

"No!"

"Is it Bonnie?"

"Un-uh!"

"How about Susan? Sherry? Wendy?"

The indignant child stomped her foot on the chair, crawled down and disgustedly marched past him to the door.

Sorry he'd teased her, Randy called, "Hey, don't leave. You haven't told me your name. I'll bet it's a nice one."

"You promise to remember?"

"Yes, I promise," Randy said. "Look, I'll even write it down." He pulled out a pen that was clipped to his shirt pocket, and the receipt for the poinsettias he'd bought earlier. Turning it over he said, "Okay. Ready."

Delighted to receive his full attention, the child walked over and whispered in his ear with painstaking precision.

Randy smiled, trying not to laugh, as he wrote it all down. "Is that it?" he asked, showing the paper for her inspection.

She giggled, clapping her hands. Then taking the paper, she folded it in half, and placed it rather ceremoniously into his pocket. Her touch was so light he hardly felt it at all. Her eyes pierced his. "Please don't forget!" she entreated him. "It's *very* important!"

"I won't forget. Absolutely not!" he promised, with a flair of sincerity and an appreciative wink.

Message accomplished, the whisp of a child climbed up into the chair next to Suzannah again. Sweetly, ever so tenderly, she touched Suzannah's cheek, leaned close to her ear, and then she yelled, *"I am here now. You can wake up and go home!"* With that, she jumped down, skipped to the door and was gone.

Astonished, Randy followed her into the hallway. To his amazement, she was already at the end of the corridor. She paused, smiled brightly, and then disappeared. He ran after her. Rounding the corner, he nearly knocked Carol down as she came from the other direction.

"Whoa, whoa. Where are you going?"

"Sorry, hon," he apologized. "Did you see a little girl run past?"

"No."

"A little blondish girl, in a white dress?"

"No. There hasn't been anybody else in the hall since I came from the elevator."

"That's weird. I could have sworn ..."

"This place is really getting to us!" Carol sympathized, taking his arm. "You're imagining things. I'm dreaming about angels."

"Dreaming angels?"

"Yeah," Carol laughed self-consciously. "It's crazy, I know. But when I dozed off in the chair this afternoon I dreamt that a heavenly angel-child came in with an important message for Suzannah. It seemed so real, but ridiculous! Anyway, sometimes you get weird dreams when you don't feel good."

"You sick?"

"Yeah. The flu probably. I was dizzy and queasy most of the day. There's must be a million germs in this place."

"And you dreamt about an angel?"

"Never mind! It was nothing. She made me promise not to forget something and told Suzannah to wake up. But Suzannah didn't wake up, and I forgot what I was supposed to remember. Definitely the strangest dream I've ever had!" Carol shook her head, embarrassed.

Randy stopped in his tracks. "Was it a name?"

"Huh? A name? I don't know. Maybe."

He took the paper out of his pocket, "Look familiar?"

Carol gasped. "That's it! Great, now I've lost my mind ... it's official! Wait a minute, how did you know?"

"You're not crazy, dear. Basically, the same thing just happened to me a few minutes ago, and it was not a dream!"

They looked at each other for a split second, then raced down the hall to Suzannah's room. Through half-open eyes, she saw them burst into the room, and smiled sleepily. It was the best Christmas gift she ever gave them!

The City. 5:23 a.m. Thursday, August 4, 1967
Suzannah's present was delivered at the Valleyhills Hospital.

Epilogue

A matronly messenger approached Ginny, who sat reading on the warm fragrant grass near the hyacinths in her favorite garden.

"How was it?" the visitor asked.

"Wonderful!" Ginny said, looking up from her book.

"How did she look?"

"So happy! And the music was as beautiful as she hoped it would be."

The messenger nodded, smiling. "I've been so pleased with your loving service, Ginny, that I wanted to bring your next assignment in person."

Ginny had expected it to be information about the next spirit child whom she would be guiding. Instead it read:

Promotion to Guardian Angel

Assignment: Kristina Celestia Evangelle 'Elan Brown

Afterword

C *hristmas Connections* came into being during a time of tremendous family difficulties, deteriorating health, and the first Christmas after the sudden death of my oldest brother, Berdell. Though he had many struggles in his own life, he had always been a balm to my sagging spirits, and an enthusiastic supporter of my writing projects. Reminiscing about holidays past, especially those of my childhood, I remembered that when I was ten years old, I had lost a specially purchased Christmas gift—a package of hankies. I began to wonder what had happened to them, who had found them, if they had been used as a gift, or for personal need. From that thought *Christmas Connections* began to develop. It seemed as if I was watching a movie and writing down the scenes as I saw them. But it was by no means a fast-moving project.

Thankfully we were able to get a computer a year later, which made all the difference to the completion of *Christmas Connections*. Often when I was unable to sleep, I could focus on the story, what my characters were feeling, saying, etc., and put in a small-town, 1960s America setting, much like the one I grew up in.

The first time that I thought it was finished, a few friends read it and liked it enough to encourage me. I sent it to a supposedly reputable editing service and shortly after they received my manuscript and requested a large sum of money, they went out of business. Luckily, I was able to stop payment on the check. This happened another time, and I grew to distrust writing-linked professionals, and to doubt my story's future.

About the third year, I started to revise the story. My

cousin, Lola, told me about a book called, *The Christmas Box* and the success it was having. I was encouraged to try again. When I felt it was completed at this stage, a couple of family members read it and helped with editing. I sent it to three publishers and was of course—rejected.

Over a year later I decided to try again. Two new characters came into being, and the heavenly-connection tying the book together was formed. It didn't change the original story, just added another dimension. Then just as I was ready to do the last edit and spell check, my Word Perfect file melted down! It happened just as I was saving changes to disc, so my good disc copy was corrupted too. All I had left of the story was a copy without any of the last three month's revisions. Of course I felt sorry for myself, and began to listen to others who said, perhaps it was God's way of saying, "It's not your turn." Or, "It's not your time." I put the book away for two years. Then we moved to Alaska.

I can't remember why I decided to try again. Maybe I was prompted by the success of others. Or, maybe I was getting a boot from the other side. This time I began each writing opportunity with prayer, knowing that I would stand a better chance of succeeding with God in my corner. I tried to find moments to write that were the least contentious in my home, and played inspirational music softly in the background.

Did it work 100 percent? No. Did it create instantaneous harmony within my family? No. But it certainly helped! It also got me back on track whenever I walked away in frustration.

During one of those times, I began praying to know if I was supposed to continue. I wondered if I was being selfish or if the timing still wasn't right. A couple of days later, I went to a special church gathering at the temple. I went with the writing question in mind, but only secondarily. Mostly my focus was on the meeting. Then an interesting thing happened.

Instead of lingering afterward to visit with other church members, as I usually would have done, I felt like I should leave. I rationalized … there is nothing pending at home, no one in dire need, why shouldn't I stay and enjoy visiting? The more I questioned this feeling, the stronger it got … leave. I did, but not with any great haste.

I stepped outside, again questioning why I had felt

prompted to leave. No answer came. A woman was parked in front of the building, waiting for her husband. I noticed an old bumper sticker from my hometown, Riverton, Utah, and began to talk to her. It turned out that she had lived in Riverton but had left over 40 years ago. I told her that I was new to Alaska and began asking her for suggestions on how to cook salmon. She was clearly a vast reservoir of knowledge. At this point, I decided that God must have wanted me to meet this lady so I would quit wasting fish, and I asked if I could call her. She said yes and gave me her card. I read it and gasped—she and her husband own the biggest publishing company in Alaska. There was my answer … go forth, it is time. I worked on my manuscript for another two months, and then just as I was ready to submit it … the entire computer melted down, and not even the computer experts could put that dumpty back together again.

This time I had a back-up copy and after the UPS man delivered our new computer, I started the final edit. Or so I thought. Through the publisher I was introduced to a real live editor, Marthy Johnson. She is the Hope Diamond in world of cut-glass editors that I had previously worked with, and a great teacher. My story lost hundreds of words on the Marthy Johnson editing diet. But *Christmas Connections* is better for it.

So, it all ends happily ever after? Not quite yet. I have learned that there is more to writing and publishing than I ever imagined, and feel like I have just stepped off the merry-go-round and bought a ticket for the roller coaster. So hang on . . .

I received a lot of help at different stages and freely acknowledge this with tremendous gratitude. What I hope now is that people who read my book will come away saying, "What a hoot!" and want to read the next book in the series. But most importantly, I hope that as you read *Christmas Connections* you will gain a renewed sense that our earthly experience is not a random happenstance or a cruel joke, but rather a planned, blessed event with eternal consequences that connect us in this world and beyond …

~ Halene ~